I WILL STAND WITH MY FATHER

ALSO BY IRENE UTTENDORFSKY

HISTORICAL FICTION:

A Punkeyville Girl: A Tale of Old Forestport and the Canals

Hannah and the Two Sisters: An Erie Canal Adventure

When Thunder Rolls, The Underground Railroad and the Civil War

CHAPTER BOOKS FOR YOUNG READERS:

Adirondack Mouse and the Perilous Journey
(Best Children's Book 2006, Adirondack Center for Writing)

Adirondack Mouse and the Mysterious Disappearance

BOARD GAME:

Adirondack's Adventure

I WILL STAND WITH MY FATHER

By

IRENE UTTENDORFSKY

ILLUSTRATIONS

BY

ALLEN A. KRAEGER

SPRUCE GULCH PRESS

BOX 4347

ROME, NY

13442

This is a work of fiction. While every effort has been made to maintain cultural and historical accuracy, the characters, dialogue, and events are either fictional or are used in an imaginary way.

Published by Spruce Gulch Press
Rome, NY, 13442

Printed by
Graphics of Utica

ISBN- 13: 978-0-984 1259-1-3
ISBN-10: 0-984 1259-1-4

FOR THE UNKNOWN PATRIOTS OF THE
AMERICAN REVOLUTIONARY WAR,
WITH THE HOPE THAT ONE DAY THEIR SACRIFICES
WILL BE KNOWN, HONORED AND REMEMBERED.

CONTENTS

PREFACE

On August 11, 2002, I attended a First American Cultural Festival: Honoring Veterans, at the Oneida Nation Homelands in Canastota, New York. The American and the Oneida re-enactors were impressive in their period clothing and weaponry, but it was when an Oneida warrior explained why his nation chose to side with the Americans rather than the British that the idea for this book was born.

The Oneidas understood that by making this choice they would have to fight against the other Iroquois Nations in a costly war with an uncertain outcome. Even if the Americans won, the Oneidas, and the Tuscaroras who fought beside them, faced a dangerous and doubtful future. Their villages and homelands would almost certainly be invaded, and many lives lost. In the end, no matter who won or lost, there was no guarantee of protection or reward for their generation. The decision to support the Americans in the Revolutionary War was made after long and careful consideration – not choosing what was best for the Oneidas at that time, but for the seventh generation.

We all make sacrifices, but how many of us would risk everything we had for people we could never know? I had to tell their story.

I am indebted to The Oneida Nation for permission to reference their website, www.oneidaindiannation.com; to the Rome Historical Society and the Fort Stanwix National Monument for their help with my early research; to William Sawyer, Park Ranger and Kandice Watson, Education and Cultural Outreach Director for the Oneida Indian Nation, for sharing their knowledge and expertise of the people, places and events of 1777, and for helping me remain true to the culture and history that formed and moved my story; to Alan Sterling for his help in obtaining a copy of the map of the Siege of Fort Schuyler, and for sharing his extensive knowledge of that place and time; to Kandice Watson and Alan Sterling for their thoughtful reviews; to Allen Kraeger for bringing life to my story with his imaginative illustrations; to my readers: Liam, Ryan and Adriana, for their helpful comments and suggestions; to JoAnn, Liana and Sue, fellow authors and members of The Wish Upon a Word Writer's Group for their insightful critiques and support; to my daughter, Susan, for her diligent editing; to Pat Langendorf, owner, Spruce Gulch Press for believing in me and my books; and to Ski, for many years of loving patience.

IROQUOIS COUNTRY, 1776

MOHAWK

West Cana

ler
)

iskany

I A N FLATS

Little Falls

Stone Arabia

Johnstown

Tribes Hill

Fort Johnson

ort Dayton

Mohawk

Fort Johnson

rt Herkimer

Fort Hunter

Springfield

Canajoharie

River

Otsego
Lake

Cherry Valley

Warren's Bush

Schenectady

Durlach

Cobleskill

Schoharie

Albany

Harpersfield

Schoharie River

Hudson River

CATSKILL
MOUNTAINS

Delaware River

Kingston

□ Fort

△ Indian settlement

● Towns

- - Fort Stanwix Treaty Line of 1768

Minisink

Newburgh

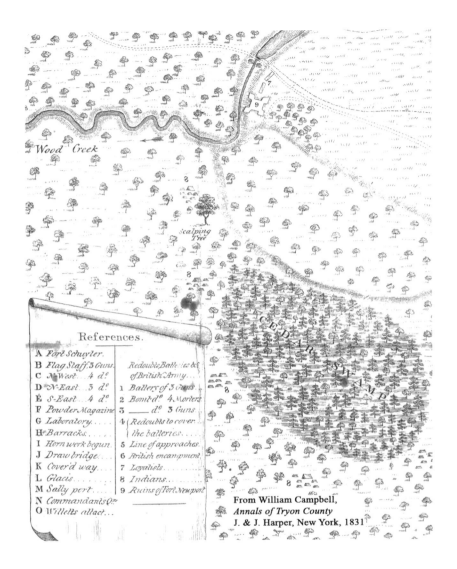

References.

A *Fort Schuyler.*
B *Flag Staff, 5 Guns.*
C *N-West....4 d.º*
D *N-East....5 d.º*
E *S-East....4 d.º*
F *Powder Magazine*
G *Laboratory......*
H *Barracks.......*
I *Horn work begun.*
J *Draw bridge....*
K *Cover'd way....*
L *Glacis........*
M *Sally port....*
N *Commandants Q.ʳ*
O *Willets attact...*

Redoubt, Batteries &c
of British Army...
1 *Battery of 5 Guns.*
2 *Bomb d.º 4 Morters*
3 ____ *d.º 3 Guns*
4 { *Redoubts to cover*
    { *the batteries....*
5 *Line of approaches.*
6 *British encampment.*
7 *Loyalists.....*
8 *Indians.....*
9 *Ruins of Fort Newport*

Wood Creek

scalping Tree

CEDAR SWAMP

From William Campbell,
Annals of Tryon County
J. & J. Harper, New York, 1831

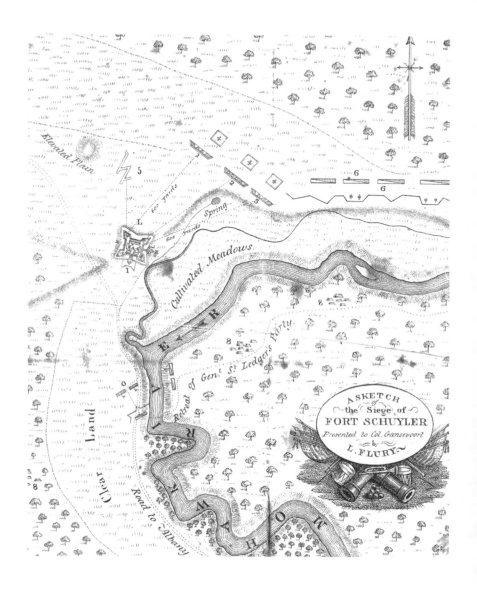

A SKETCH of the Siege of FORT SCHUYLER Presented to Col. Gansevoort by L. FLURY

I WILL STAND WITH MY FATHER

BOOK ONE

August 1st – August 7th

1777

"It is the unalterable resolution of the Oneidas and Tuscaroras, at every hazard, to hold fast the Covenant Chain with the United States, and with them be buried in the same grave; or to enjoy the fruits of victory and peace."

An Oneida Chief[1]

1

CHAPTER 1

THE SIGN

I ran with a heavy heart and clumsy feet, like a wounded deer trying to outrun the hunter. Still, I raced toward the American fort with my friend, Tracking Wolf, and Paul Powless, famed runner of Oriska. Two days ago Paul had carried the letter from our sachems to Colonel Gansevoort; the letter that pulled us into the boiling pot of the American's rebellion. Now we hurried to warn Gansevoort that St. Leger's army had already invaded our country and his soldiers were now on the march to attack the fort.

"May the spirit of Quiver Bearer forgive us for destroying the League," I said.[1]

Tracking Wolf grinned. "Skyholder sent us a good day for our first express run, Walks on Snow," he said. "With no rain or wind to slow us down, our feet can fly."

I frowned. "How can you smile? What we are doing today can never be undone."

He laughed. "I'm happy to feel the sun on my back. That's a good omen sent by orenda, or, perhaps, by Reverend Kirkland's God."

"Don't talk to me about the sun," I said. "It bloodied the dawn this morning, like the tomahawks of our brother Mohawks stained the scalps of those American girls a few days ago.[2] I shuddered when those bloody fingers reached out for our homes in Kanonwalohale and colored the heavens over the carry and the fort."

Tracking Wolf snorted. "Skyholder always sets red paint in the sky to warn that a storm will come soon," he said. "It won't come today."

"I tell you a different kind of storm is brewing," I said. "My fingers prickled as I oiled my scalp lock with bear grease and placed my eagle feathers. I can't forget that evil omen."

"We're nearing the fort," Paul said as he sprinted past us. "Keep your mind on our mission."

His words stung. "Does he think we're children?"

Tracking Wolf shrugged.

As my moccasins skimmed over the uneven ground the rhythm of the run quieted my mind. Although the hot summer sun bore down on us, the breeze we made as we ran cooled my skin, bare except for my loincloth and the musket slung over my back. Tall grasses bowed down as we raced by them.

"This is not our fight," I said. "We should not have chosen sides."

"The Grand Council fire at Onondagas no longer burns," Tracking Wolf said. "Each nation had to decide where they would stand."[3] He set his jaw. "I'm glad we chose the Americans. They love freedom, just as we do."

"But the English offer money and promise to protect our homeland."

Tracking Wolf snorted. "So did William Johnson. How much land did he take from us and sell for money we never saw?"

I shook my head. "We still should have stayed neutral."

"How could we after yesterday? Our Iroquois brothers rejected every one of our arguments for peace at Three Rivers. They chose to side with the British."

"So we, the People of the Standing Stone, must fight all the other nations of the League of the Haudenosaunee?"

Tracking Wolf didn't answer. When Paul disappeared around a bend in the path, Tracking Wolf sprinted after him.

I pumped my legs faster until I caught up with him. As we ran together in stride I scanned the road ahead. All of a sudden Paul skidded to a halt.

I raised a hand to signal Tracking Wolf and stopped running. Quick as a striking snake he yanked me behind a tree.

A tall Mohawk stepped out from the underbrush a few feet beyond Paul. He wore a red woolen vest over his linen shirt and British trousers above his leggings.

My heart pounded my chest. "That's Joseph Brant," I whispered.

Paul turned toward the underbrush, like he wanted to bolt into the woods.

"Halt!" Brant shouted.

Paul turned back. He faced Joseph Brant with his musket raised.

CHAPTER 2

THE KING'S MESSAGE

Joseph Brant held out his hand, like a friend. "I give you my word," he said to Paul. "You will not be harmed or held captive. I only wish to speak with you."[1]

I didn't hear truth in his words. My thoughts darted here and there like a rabbit trying to find a way out of the snare. Paul stood tall in the face of great danger.

"We can't hide ourselves like women," I whispered. "We have to let Brant see that Paul is not alone."

Tracking Wolf nodded.

I took a deep breath. The strong odor of pine pitch braced my resolve. I stepped out from behind the gnarled white pine, symbol of our peace but no longer our refuge. I pointed my musket at Joseph Brant. At my side, Tracking Wolf did the same.

Joseph Brant didn't move or change his expression. His eyes flickered with distrust when they met mine. He lifted his hand. Four armed Mohawks appeared from the woods behind him as if by magic.

"Come closer if you want to give me a message," Paul said to Brant. "But come alone." His finger twitched on the trigger.

Brant took a step forward. "My message is from the king," he said. "He offers you his protection."

"That's close enough," Paul said. "What else does the king say?"

I leaned forward. Would the king promise to protect our homeland if we swore to remain neutral? If he did, maybe our chiefs would accept his offer and turn us away from this war.

"The king offers rich rewards for your loyalty," Brant said. His words flowed off his tongue like sweet honey from an open hive. "He has plenty money for you if you convince your brother

Oneidas to stand with the king and help his soldiers take the fort."

My faint hope faded. There would be no reward if we simply vowed not to take sides. Why couldn't the king see that this would be better, for him and for us? We would promise not to interfere in his fight with the settlers if he allowed us to hunt, fish and trap to prepare our village for the famine of the coming winter.

"No longer will the Oneidas have to hunt beaver to sell to white men," Brant said, as if he had read my mind. "If you swear your allegiance to the British king he will give you all the money you need to live in peace with your Iroquois brothers."

Why couldn't the British and the Americans leave us out of their war? All I wanted was the freedom to hunt and roam freely through Iroquois country, with no boundaries or barriers – and no more settlers coming to lay claim to our lands.

Paul lifted his chin. "My brother Oneidas and I have joined our fortunes with the Americans. We will share with them whatever good or ill may come of that."

I flinched. Did he want to make us the first to die?

A blue jay screamed a warning. The rich scents of pine, hemlock and spruce rose up from the woods. The soft, green forest surrounded us like a shield, but raw danger raised a net and stood poised to snare us. My heart raced. Every muscle of my body shouted, "Run!" But I stood firm and steadied my musket.

Joseph Brant's eyes flashed with anger. "I do not wish my Oneida brothers any harm," he said. "But heed my warning. Change the minds of your fellow Oneidas before it's too late. The English king has great and relentless power. He will bring about the ruin of your nation if you fight against him."

Now he spoke the truth. Many more soldiers fought in the king's army, and the British soldiers were better trained and more experienced in warfare than the Americans. If the American patriots lost this war, we would be branded traitors to the British cause. How would the king deal with us then?

"As long as one of us is left standing, the Oneida people will never turn their backs on the Americans," Paul said. Then he bolted into the forest.

Tracking Wolf raced after him. I sprinted through the underbrush to catch up, weaving in and out between the trees, darting around fallen limbs and vaulting over the trunks of blow-downs.

Musket fire punctuated the angry shouts and shrieks of the Mohawks who chased us. We burst out of the forest and sped down the road that led to the fort.

When old Fort Stanwix rose up from the earth just ahead of us, relief smothered the hot flames of my fear. The fort's solid earthworks and ring of sharpened sticks they called "fraise" stood ready to protect us. All we had to do was to get inside, and we would be safe.

I drew a sharp breath. The drawbridge had been lifted, blocking that way inside. Paul hesitated for just a moment and then dashed toward the side wall of the fort.

"He's heading for the sally-port!" I shouted to Tracking Wolf.

Tracking Wolf sprinted after Paul with me on his heels. More enemy musket powder exploded behind us. Their shot pinged against trees and thunked the ground behind us. A cannon on the northeast bastion boomed. Oneida pickets outside the fort fired back at the Mohawks who still chased us.

"Look sharp!" an American soldier called from the parapet above us. "There's Indians headed for the sally-port. Stand by to repel the invaders!"

Startled, I glanced toward the sally-port. All I could see were the American soldiers manning the redoubt, and Paul running straight at them.

"Just a few more paces and we'll be inside," Tracking Wolf called back to me.

Musket fire erupted from the parapet. A musket ball buried itself in the dirt near Tracking Wolf's foot. He kept running.

I skidded to a stop and looked up at the parapet. Black smoke curled from the barrel of an American soldier's musket. The soldier next to him aimed his weapon at me.

"Halt or be shot!" a soldier at the redoubt shouted to Paul.

Stunned, my mind reeled, my legs faltered. After fifteen summers, would this day be my last?

CHAPTER 3

THE FORT

Musket balls peppered the fort's wall and the grassy berm behind me.[1] Black powder tainted the air. Paul dropped to the ground and rolled closer to the wall. The American soldier on the parapet kept his musket trained on me.

"Let us in!" Paul shouted to the soldiers manning the redoubt. "We bring news for your colonel."

The soldier who had shot at Tracking Wolf shoved a ramrod down the barrel of his gun to set a charge for me. I dived toward the wall and rolled under the fraise.

"Hold fire!" Jacob Doxtator, son of our warrior, Hanyery, shouted from the parapet.[2] "These are Oneidas, come to help you. Let them in before their message falls into the hands of the British or their Mohawks."

"Open the sally-port," Captain Jansen shouted.

The soldiers at the redoubt turned their weapons away from us and fired a round at the Mohawks behind us.

I bolted for the sally-port. An enemy ball struck the ground a few paces behind me.

Tracking Wolf grabbed my arm and pulled me around the redoubt. "Where were you?" he shouted.

"Trying to stay alive," I said. "We risked our lives to bring them information and this is how they repay us?" My blood boiled. I shook my fist at the soldiers on the parapet.

Tracking Wolf stuck out his chest and grinned. "We must have looked like a pack of war-crazed warriors to them."

"That's not funny," I said as we jogged into the long outer building of the sally-port. "They would have killed us if Jacob hadn't been there to stop them."

When the door to the fort swung open, we ran onto the parade ground. Paul headed toward Colonel Gansevoort's quarters.

"Halt!" an American soldier shouted. He stepped in front of Paul.

"We bring information about the British Army," Paul said. "The colonel must hear our message right away."

The soldier lowered his musket, but he looked wary. "The colonel is a mite busy," he said. "Give me the message. I'll see to it that he gets it."

"That won't be necessary, Private Jones," Colonel Gansevoort said as he stepped up behind the soldier. "Tell Lieutenant Colonel Willett he is to come at once to the staff room." He turned to Paul. "Come with me to my quarters."

"There is more," Paul said. He pulled out our wampum belt. "We bring you this belt to prove the truth of our words."

Gansevoort took the belt. His stern eyes swept over us, questioning and wary.

I bristled. We came here to help, wasn't that enough to earn his trust? Did he think we were British spies?

Gansevoort blinked. "Take these men to the storehouse," he ordered. "Give them a ration of bread and water so they can refresh themselves after their run."

Private Jones presented his musket, stock down and barrel up in salute. He held his body as stiff as a ramrod. Colonel Gansevoort returned the salute and then stomped toward the staff room with Paul close behind.

Private Jones headed toward the southeast bastion. A sweep of his hand signaled us to follow him.

I glared at his back. I didn't need anyone to lead me to the storehouse. I had come to old Fort Stanwix many times with my father, Eagle Tail. So what if the Americans changed the name to Fort Schuyler? [3] I still knew how to get to the storehouse.

We passed the soldiers barracks in the casemate

Paul presents the wampum belt

of the sally-port and headed for the southeast bastion. The aroma of fresh-baked bread drew me into the storehouse. Once inside, Private Jones handed each of us a piece of bread. He drew a small bucket of water from a barrel and set it down in front of us before he walked away.

"I could have found the storehouse with my eyes closed," I said.

Tracking Wolf laughed. "You could have followed your nose."

"Colonel Gansevoort only sent an escort with us because he doesn't trust us. Why do we bother to bring him information he probably doesn't believe?"

Tracking Wolf shook his head. "Are you sure it's Gansevoort who lacks trust? Maybe he sent a guide to his gift of food as a sign of friendship." He grinned. "Or perhaps the colonel has heard about your appetite and fears for his store of bread."

I scowled and took a bite of the crusty bread. It tasted salty and sweet at the same time, not anything like the tasty corn bread my mother made. I sipped a handful of water from the bucket and made a face. Once, this water had bubbled fresh and pure in the sally-port spring outside the fort. Now it tasted musty and foul from being trapped in the soldiers' water barrel.

I looked up as Paul came into the storehouse. "Will the colonel give an answer for us to bring back to Chief Skenandoah?" I asked.

Paul looked over his shoulder. "If he has an answer, we will not have long to wait."

Jacob joined us from the parapet. "What message did you bring?" he asked. "What are the words from the council at Kanonwalohale?"

"It's been two days since the council urged Colonel Gansevoort to stand firm against the British and their Indians," I said. "We came to tell him that the enemy outside the fort is only a small part of the king's plan. They were sent ahead of the main army to prepare to lay siege. St. Leger is on his way with a much larger force of soldiers and Indians. They are no more than four hours away by now."

Jacob looked disgusted. "There is much confusion here," he said. "But at least the Americans have taken some actions to protect themselves. They have felled trees into Wood Creek to prevent the enemy from using that route to bring in their heavy guns. But they still haven't finished rebuilding the northeast bastion. If more soldiers don't come to help them defend that part, this fort will fall, like Ticonderoga."

A spattering of musket fire erupted outside the fort. The battle seemed more distant now that we were inside, but the consequences of our alliance with the Americans loomed even larger in my mind. As the soldiers on the parapet returned fire, I pictured my village in flames, my mother and sister screaming as they ran from British soldiers. I blinked to clear my head of that awful image.

"I offered my services to the fort as messenger," Paul said. "I will slip away after dark tonight and find a mount. Then I'll ride south to bring news of the enemy siege to the American forces there."[4]

Jacob nodded. "My mother, Two Kettles Together, has already left the fort. She goes first to Oriska and from there she will ride to Fort Dayton and beyond to spread the word. She brings along a copy of the letter from your sachems to General Herkimer. We hope he will call up the local militia and bring them here to help us hold the fort."

"But will he come in time?" Tracking Wolf asked as we climbed up to the parapet.

"The question is will he come at all?" I said. "My father says General Herkimer's loyalty is questioned by some. His brother, Joost, remains loyal to the king and fights with the British.[5] How do we know the general's heart is with the Americans?"

"We have to believe he's with us," Jacob said. "If he chose to side with the loyalists, he would have gone with his brother to join St. Leger."

"Send more men to the northeast bastion!" an American officer shouted. "The enemy is launching an attack there at our weakest point. They may breech the wall!"

"We can't let that happen," Paul said. He loped away in that direction.

I looked out from the parapet. The British Indians crouched behind trees and bushes and sniped at the soldiers on the parapet. As soon as an Indian discharged his musket, the Americans returned fire. While the soldiers reloaded, other Indians darted from their hiding places and took cover closer to the fort.

Our Oneida pickets, as skilled in Indian warfare as the Mohawks, kept up a steady fire to keep them from reaching the walls. The smoke and the smell of black powder muddied the air. By the position of the sun it was about mid-afternoon.

"Where is your father?" Jacob asked.

"Eagle Tail left for Oriska with Thomas Spencer this morning before sunrise," I said. "They will council with the sachems and chiefs there. They hope to rally support for the Americans who will come here to help defend the fort."

Jacob nodded. "We will need many more soldiers when St. Leger arrives with the rest of his army. Our scouts have told us he brings over a thousand fighting men, including hundreds of Iroquois warriors."

I looked away. What would Jacob think if he knew I wanted no part in this? I didn't want to be a loyalist or a patriot. I didn't want Oneida blood to be spilled on either side in this war. But here we stood, alone on the brink of our own destruction, caught between two opposing armies.

I silently cursed them all: William Johnson and his treachery, Samuel Kirkland and his God and the Americans with their tempting ways. Without them we could have continued to live in peace with our brothers.

"Look sharp!" an American soldier shouted. "A whole passel of Indians is holed up in yonder barn." He pointed toward a farm the local settlers had abandoned when they were sent away for their safety after the attack on the young girls. He raised his musket and fired a shot in that direction.

Indians fired back from hiding places inside and around the barn. Even our Oneida pickets fell back and took cover from these clever enemies.

I raised my musket and fired at them. They whooped and laughed as they capered in and out of their fortress. More Indians took refuge in a second barn and joined the fight.

"I'm shot!" a soldier on the parapet yelled. He dropped his musket and grabbed his arm. Blood oozed between his fingers.

"Take that man to the hospital!" Lieutenant Colonel Willett shouted. "Private Jones to the parapet in his stead."

After a while daylight faded. The guns of both sides slowly fell silent. On the parade ground below us a group of soldiers gathered.

"The Americans must be planning a raid," I said.

Paul and Jacob jumped down from the parapet and ran to join them.

The fire of war flickered in Tracking Wolf's dark eyes. He didn't seem to notice the doubt smoldering in mine.

He grabbed my arm. "Come on!" he said, pulling me along. "We don't want to be left behind."

CHAPTER 4
WAR PAINT

A short time later I sat on the dry, dusty ground near the wall of the southeast casemate with my Oneida friends.

"This raid is a good plan," Tracking Wolf said. He bit off a piece of dried deer meat and chewed slowly. "You saw how the enemy Indians used those barns against us. Something must be done about that."

I grunted agreement. At least this battle would be waged like our own, using surprise and the cover of darkness to strike a quick blow against the enemy and then withdraw.[1]

My stomach complained of hunger. I wet my fingers with spit and poked them into my pouch of parched corn. I sucked the sweet, powdered corn from my fingers and reached for more.

Paul dipped his finger into black face-paint and smeared it over one side of his face. He painted the rest of his face deep blue. "When the raid begins I will slip through the British lines," he said. "I'll take one of their horses and ride off before they even know I'm there."

I gulped stale water from my cupped hand to wash down the dry corn. "Take care that you don't run afoul of St. Leger's soldiers," I said.

"Walks on Snow is right," Jacob said as he drew jagged red stripes across his cheek. "St. Leger must be close to the fort by now. If you're captured or killed before you can tell the American patriots at Schenectady that we need their help, this fort will fall."

Paul grunted. A spark of anger flashed in his eyes. "You can be sure that I will be in Schenectady long before St. Leger knows I came through his lines."

I glanced at the sky. Gathering clouds chased the twilight and beckoned to the darkness. With any luck those clouds would cover the face of the young moon. "I see Skyholder's spirit at work," I said. "He'll draw his cloud curtain tonight and shield us with darkness."

Paul nodded. He handed me a paint pot. "You need to honor your warrior father by painting your face."

I smeared my face with blue paint and thought about my father. He had often spoken of the eloquent speech Thomas Spencer made two years ago at Cherry Valley. Thomas' words had so inspired the settlers that they picked up their guns and joined the fight for liberty. He should have no trouble convincing our own people at Oriska to go to help Herkimer and the soldiers coming from Fort Dayton. Would my father and Thomas go with them?

Suddenly, a hand slapped my back. I grabbed my tomahawk and whirled to face my attacker.

"You can be sure that I will be in
Schenectady long before St. Leger knows . ..

Tracking Wolf's eyes laughed at me in the fading light. "It's good that you hold yourself ready to fight," he said. "But I will live longer if you look before you reach for your tomahawk."

Tension drained from my arm as I lowered my weapon. "I should have known it was you," I said. "You always take delight in sneaking up on me. No wonder your mother chose 'Bolt from the Sky' for your child name. She said you took the spirit of a brave warrior before you left her womb."

He grinned as he pulled me to my feet. "Somebody has to wake you from your dreams of Polly," he said. "It's time to prepare our torches."

I scowled. "I wasn't thinking of her."

Tracking Wolf chuckled. "Perhaps you should. "You're not the only warrior who's noticed her beauty."

Before I could ask if he spoke of himself or someone else, he darted into the soldiers barracks.

Annoyed, I followed him. By the time my eyes adjusted to the dimmer light in the barracks, Tracking Wolf had already pulled a handful of straw from the long crib where the soldiers slept.

"Jacob went out the sally-port to cut some green wood," he said. "This dry straw will feed our torch flames well."

I yanked a big wad of straw from the crib and followed Tracking Wolf outside. A group of soldiers had gathered near the sally-port.

A faint knock, followed by the soft coo of a dove came from the other side of the heavy door. I held my breath as the soldiers swung the door open a crack, and then wider.

Jacob slipped inside, his arms full of thick branches, limbed and leafless.

Tracking Wolf stepped forward and grabbed a sturdy limb. A shiver of excitement rippled the back of my neck as I picked a stout bough.

"Ready your torches," Captain Jansen said. "When you hear two cannon on the southwest bastion fire, we go."

"Why do you set off the cannon?" I asked one of the Massachusetts soldiers.

"Captain says the noise and the grapeshot will scare off any Indians still hiding in the barns," he said. "That way they won't be able to ambush us before we can set the fires."

I snorted. If they thought that one or two cannon shots would scatter brave Iroquois warriors, they had much to learn about the art of Indian warfare.

BOOM!

The report of the first cannon echoed in my ears as I bound the straw to my stick with a leather thong. Despite my misgivings, the beguiling fever of war awakened and coursed through my blood.

"Stay together," Captain Jansen said. "Form a line, single file through the sally-port."

"What about the Indians?" one of the soldiers asked. He glanced over his shoulder at my painted face. "How do we know we can trust them not to turn on us when we get outside?"

"They should go out first," Private Jones said. "That way they can't sneak up on us."

A spurt of anger loosened my tongue. "We pledged to help you," I said. "You accepted our wampum belt as proof of our friendship, yet you accuse us of treachery?"

"No," Captain Jansen said. "We're just not sure your passion for our cause is strong enough for you to stand against your Iroquois brothers in battle."

Paul's eyes darkened and widened in his painted face. "Our chiefs and sachems have considered all these things," he said. "We are prepared to do whatever we can to help you."

Paul's words hung in the silence that followed. I moved closer to the soldiers who were crouched by the sally-port door. I inclined my head to Private Jones. He nodded and motioned me closer to his back.

BOOM!

CHAPTER 5

THE RAID

We ran through the sally-port with the sound of the last cannon shot still ringing in our ears. I fixed my eyes on Private Jones' back and matched his stride as we snaked toward the outer door.

I gulped a breath of cool air as I burst out into the night and ran behind the guard at the redoubt. I bent low to the ground, keeping my body close to the dark, concealing grasses. I darted around the slower soldiers, and let my feet fly over the rough ground. Jacob and Tracking Wolf ran at either side of me. Paul sprinted past, headed for the British lines.

We made almost no sound as we raced through the grass and rounded the northeast bastion. The soldiers tried to be quiet. They had wrapped the wheels of their field piece in cloth, but the muffled thumps and groans the big gun made as it lurched through ruts and bumped over stones tainted the hushed night.

Suddenly shadowy shapes ran at us from the wooded area up ahead. Were they allies or enemy Indians? I clenched my tomahawk, ready to defend myself if it came to that.

The coo of a dove sounded from their direction. Jacob gave the answering call. I relaxed my grip on my weapon and let go of my breath. These Indians must be Oneida pickets from outside the fort.

One of them ran up to me and matched my stride. I glanced at his painted face, a mysterious and frightful mask. But under the paint I recognized the familiar slant of his nose, the friendly look in his eye and his toothy grin.

"Stay close to the edge of the breastworks," my mother's brother, Laughing Fox, said in a low voice. "Most of the British and their Indians are camped beyond the northeast bastion. But watch out for Brant and his Mohawks. They hide nearby and wait for anyone foolish enough to cross their path."

I nodded. Joseph Brant was the last person I wanted to meet up with tonight.

Despite his age, Laughing Fox kept pace with me as I sprinted across the endless breastworks and skirted the ditch. Then we raced across the cleared land and headed for our target. The first barn loomed large and dark against a clearing sky. Above the barn's roof a few stars twinkled. Soon the moon would escape the thinning clouds and show us to the enemy.

Heavy dew dampened the grass where I dropped to my knees by the open barn door. The scents of moist earth, trampled meadow plants and wildflowers filled tickled my nose.

Laughing Fox grunted as he went down on one knee. He pulled the top from the clay pot that hung on a thong from his wrist. A twist of smoke curled up from its opening.

I yanked a few strands of straw from my torch

and poked them into the smoldering coals in the pot. Fire leapt up from the coals and hungrily licked at the dry stalks. Before the fire had time to taste my fingers, I shoved the burning straws into the hay bound to my stick. Orange flame coiled up into the dried grass. The reflection of its light danced along the metal parts of my uncle's rifle.

As soon as my torch was ablaze, I darted into the barn. Through an open window I saw the leaping lights of other flaming sticks. I shoved my hissing fire-stick into the first pile of hay I spied. My fire swallowed the hay and erupted into a crackling, smoking, hungry inferno that mounted the wall and reached for the roof timbers. My spirit rose up too, at one with the dancing flames.

A sudden blast of heat scorched my bare chest. Acrid smoke stung my eyes and scalded my throat. I coughed and staggered back from the unexpected firestorm. Desperate to flee the flames I whirled around, but I couldn't see the doorway through the thickening smoke. Panic overwhelmed me as a spark of fear singed the back of my neck. Smoke filled my nose and my lungs. I flailed my arms. My heart pounded like a giant water drum.

A firm hand clutched my elbow. "This way," my uncle said.

Like a blind man, I staggered toward the sound of his voice. Relief extinguished my fear as I stumbled out the door behind him, coughing and gasping breaths of sweet, cool air.

Flames engulfed both barns. Angry shouts drifted from the enemy camp on a quickening wind.

The American soldiers cheered. The thrill of our success filled me with pride. I held my tomahawk high and added my voice to our warrior's victory cry. Distant rifle and musket fire answered us from the British encampment.

"Return to the fort!" Captain Jansen shouted. "Gunner, give cover to the rear!"

I turned to my uncle. "It was foolish of me to stay in the barn so long," I said. I looked down so he couldn't see my shame at having to be rescued like a silly child.

Laughing Fox lifted my chin. "That was one more lesson you needed to learn," he said. His eyes met mine, soft and forgiving.

The other Oneidas melted into the shadows, some heading back toward the fort, others slipping into the woods.

Laughing Fox rested his hand on my shoulder. "Go back to the fort with your friends," he said. He slung his rifle over his shoulder. "Your mother sends me on to Oriska to fight beside your father when he joins Herkimer's army."

I took a deep breath. It was time for me to put aside my childish fear and indecision. "I will go with you to Oriska," I said. "I will stand with my father."

Laughing Fox looked surprised. "Eagle Tail said you were to remain here."

His words spoke my father's message, but the sadness in his eyes told me he would take me with him if he could.

I balled my hands into fists. Once, when I was young, I had disobeyed my father and put my own needs ahead of the survival of the clan. How much more time had to pass before I could have a chance to prove to him that I had learned from my mistake?

I snorted. "If my father keeps leaving me behind how will I ever earn his respect as a warrior?"

"Your time will come," Laughing Fox said.

I grunted. "When it is finally my turn to fight this war in earnest, can I use your fine rifle?"

Laughing Fox laughed. "I will tell your father that you need a fine rifle."

I grinned. "I have seen the rifles the sharpshooters use against us. I would be a better warrior with a gun like that."

"I will tell him," Laughing Fox said. "But for now you must take your musket back to the fort."

My shoulders drooped. "I'll stay here and defend the fort, but my heart goes to Oriska with you." I touched his arm. "Take care, Uncle. Who will rescue me from my mistakes if you fall in battle there?"

"The ohwachira will always be here for you," he said.[1] "Besides, you have already learned all that I can teach you." He chuckled. "Someday you will be called 'Uncle' by your own sister's sons."

I laughed when I tried to imagine my little sister, Two Doves, old enough to marry and have a child. All I could see in my mind was her little-girl smile as she crooned to her doll instead of stirring the stew like our mother told her to.

Laughing Fox raised his hand in farewell and then I stood alone on the open field. Flames flared and crackled within the charred remains of the barns. Up ahead, the soldiers tramped toward the fort. Their lumbering cannon drew close behind me.

I broke into a run until I caught up with the soldiers. British army campfires twinkled in the darkness beyond the fort. The last few clouds slipped past the moon as we reached the breastworks. Now we could see and be seen by the enemy.

CHAPTER 6

SURROUNDED

I bent lower to the ground and ran faster. The soldiers picked up their pace as well. A few stray shots came at us from the woods where Brant and his warriors were likely camped. The boom of the field piece answered behind us.

We poured through the sally-port, guided by the bobbing light of a lantern held high by the open door that led into the fort.

"Good work, men," Captain Jansen said as we passed through the portal.

I grinned and raised my arm in victory, even though I knew his compliment was not meant for me.

"Walks on Snow!" Tracking Wolf called. He stepped from the shadows on the parade ground and grabbed my arm. "We thought you were injured, or that you decided to go with Laughing Fox."

"My uncle goes to be with my father at Oriska," I said, glad we were headed toward the soldiers' barracks where the deep shadows would hide the disappointment I couldn't keep from my face.

"I wouldn't blame you for going with him," Tracking Wolf said.

The sour taste of wild grapes coated my tongue. "Yes," I said. "Their mission is most important to the defense of this fort. With our Oneida scouts and warriors to guide and protect them Herkimer and his soldiers will have a better chance of getting here in time to bolster Gansevoort's army."

Jacob nodded. "I'm sure our warriors will be here with Herkimer's militia soon."

I grabbed my blanket from the pile we had made of our belongings before the raid. I wrapped it around me and lay down on the ground outside the barracks.

Jacob yawned as he reclined near Tracking Wolf. "Brant and his Indians will have to find another fortress tomorrow," he said. "There's no place for them to hide in those burned barns."

"That's not the only good news," Tracking Wolf said. "The bateaus that came today brought more supplies from Fort Dayton and one hundred soldiers sent as guards."

"Too bad the bateau men lingered at the landing," I said. "Our scouts reported two wounded by the British Iroquois, one taken prisoner and one missing."

Tracking Wolf grunted. He and Jacob fell into an eager debate, examining every detail of tonight's raid.

I rolled onto my back. A cluster of stars glittered in the cloudless, velvet sky. Full-throated snores of every sound and rhythm rolled from the barracks like rumbling thunder.

Tomorrow St. Leger and the rest of his army would probably arrive to blockade the fort. He would cut off our lines of communication beyond the fort and keep any new supplies from reaching us. He and his army would bottle us up, like the water the Americans held captive in their barrels.

How long could we hold out? Until General Herkimer and his militia came to rescue us? But what if Herkimer never came? Would we die here when we ran out of food, water and ammunition?

Without warning my worst childhood fear sprang up and seized my throat. My breath rattled, my chest rose and fell but no air squeezed past the paralyzing fear that strangled me.

I willed my spirit to rise up and look down on my struggle. The fat, grey wolf tore at my throat. The gleam of the coming kill flashed in his vicious eyes, but I didn't see any hunger there – only disgust at my weakness. For an instant his jaw slackened.

With all my strength I pushed him away and gasped a breath. I opened my mouth wide and drew in another breath, and then another, each one deeper and slower than the one before. As my pinched throat loosened, air flowed in and out of my lungs. My spirit came back into my body. The wolf of starvation growled before he slunk away with his tail between his legs. He would come again when the time was right.

I rolled onto my side. Lulled by the slow, deep breaths of Tracking Wolf and Jacob, I surrendered myself to sleep.

By the time the morning sun rose on the eastern horizon, I had already finished my breakfast of parched corn and bread. I washed it down with a handful of stale water and scowled at the ramparts that kept me from my homeland.

"How long do you think it will take for Herkimer and his militia to come from Fort Dayton?" I asked.

Jacob lifted his eyes to the sky like he expected to see an answer there. "Most of the farmers who serve in the Tryon County Militia live many miles from one another. It will take several days before all of them reach Fort Dayton."[1]

"Let's go up and take a look at the enemy's position," Tracking Wolf said.

Jacob and I followed him up onto the southeast parapet. A large group of Indians and British soldiers had gathered beyond the fort. Was this more of the advance forces or had St. Leger already arrived? A sudden panic clutched at my throat, trapping my breath like a rabbit in a snare.

"The enemy has strengthened," I said. "Soon we will have no means to get away from here."

Jacob looked surprised. "We're supposed to stay here and support the Americans," he said. "Unless we're sent out to forage for food or gather and carry information, we have no reason to leave."

I pulled in a breath of cool morning air. The tightness in my throat eased as I raised my face to the sun. "You're right," I said.

A drummer sounded the call to assemble. "Hold your stations on the parapet!" the captain shouted.

I looked down inside the fort. Soldiers ran out onto the parade ground from all directions. They halted and stood at attention.

Colonel Gansevoort walked back and forth in front of them. "Here at Fort Schuyler we have been entrusted with a sacred duty," he said. "Upon your shoulders rests the future of this young nation. We are now surrounded on all sides by the enemy. This fort is all that stands between them and certain victory in the valley. If they overpower us, there will be nothing to stop them from taking all of New York. We must hold fast to Fort Schuyler. We must endure the hardships of siege for as long as it takes. We must never give up the fight for our freedom and for our children's freedom."

And for our freedom, too, I thought. If the Americans lose this war, so will the Oneidas. We have no choice left, but to help them win.

Tracking Wolf pointed to the southeast bastion. "Look," he said.

A flag inched up the flagpole there. Red, white and blue cloth fluttered in the light morning breeze.[2] The fife and drum played. The soldiers faced the flagpole.

"This is your new flag, the standard of our liberty," Gansevoort said. "You must defend these colors at all costs."

I shook my head. The only liberty they had won so far was the right to occupy this fort. But beyond these walls the whole British army prepared to lay siege, to crush them and destroy their yearning to be free. Without our help, the redcoats and their allies would overrun the fort's defenses and kill all the Americans. Then the British would come looking for us.

I raised my musket in salute to their flag. I would stand with my father. I would fight alongside the Americans and defend their right to be free of British rule. I could only hope that we would reap the same rewards when the victory dance ended.

A cannon aimed at the main enemy camp boomed. The fife and drum signaled the end of the flag raising ceremony.

I turned and looked out toward the Mohawk River, across the cleared land and along the road that disappeared into the forest beyond.

"Do you think this garrison will hold long enough to see Herkimer's militia march down that road to our rescue?" I asked.

"Maybe," Tracking Wolf said. "But the enemy doesn't look concerned. See how their Indians boldly stroll among the trees at the edge of the forest?"

"The British and German soldiers strut and swagger at will," Jacob said. "Time is their ally, not ours. All they have to do is wait for us to surrender."

I shook my head. "I hope I don't live to see that day."

When the sun hung near the middle of the sky, we tramped down from the parapet. Eager to feed my hunger and slake my thirst I ran all the way to the storehouse.

Tracking Wolf laughed when he caught up with me. "I pity the poor British soldier who comes between Walks on Snow and his food," he said.

I grabbed my stomach to quiet a mournful squeal. "At least for today I will not die of starvation," I said. Somewhere deep in the forest a wolf howled as I choked down another bite of bread.

Jacob chuckled. "Walks on Snow runs on swift feet when he's hungry," he said. "If the British keep us here until the food runs out, he will single-handedly overpower them and eat all of their stores." He and Tracking Wolf shrieked with laughter.

My cheeks burned. "We need to keep up our strength for battle," I said. "This is not the time to fast and dream."

"That depends on who you dream about," Tracking Wolf said. He threw back his head and laughed louder.

I shot him an angry look and took another bite of bread. "I only dream of the coming fight."

"Somebody needs to protect Gansevoort's stores from Walks on Snow," Jacob said. "If this warrior is allowed to satisfy his bottomless hunger, the Americans may have to surrender before another morning comes."

I turned my back and chewed on a piece of dried venison. They don't know what it's like to be hunted by the wolf of starvation, I thought. I stuffed the rest of my bread into my mouth and swallowed it whole.

My belly felt satisfied, but my mind still craved food. I closed my eyes so I didn't have to watch my friends eat.

Suddenly I was back home again. The aroma of the bubbling rabbit stew my mother had been cooking on that crisp day last fall made my mouth water. The sweetness of her fried corn bread and honey had danced on my tongue since breakfast. Now the spirits of the two sisters, squash and bean, swam together in my bowl, and under the cooking fire's hot coals roasted the third sister, corn. I pushed back the coals with a stick and cautiously grabbed one steaming hot ear. I peeled back the husk and chewed on the tender, smoky kernels.

Long before this corn grew plump and full on the stalk, the Green Corn Ceremony had been celebrated with corn pudding made from the young milk-corn to honor the first ears. My heart thumped as I recalled that sunny day last summer when Polly shared a bowl of her sweet corn pudding with me. My face burned as I recalled her dark eyes and sweet smile. I got to my feet and strode to the water barrel. A gulp of musty water dampened my longing for food.

"We'll all have to get used to eating less food unless Herkimer and his men get here soon," Tracking Wolf said.

"This year our people will suffer more hunger in the time of little food," Jacob said.

"Especially if the enemy destroys our crops before the harvest," I said. "And even if that doesn't happen, how will we prepare for the coming winter if we can't go on the fall hunt because we have to fight this war?"

Suddenly the drummer beat the alarm. Soldiers swarmed to their posts. Tracking Wolf, Jacob and I ran up to the parapet along the southeast bastion. The American's shouted and pointed to the east.

A small group of Gansevoort's men ran toward the sally-port from the direction of the upper landing on the Mohawk not far from the ruins of old Fort Craven. Enemy Indians pursued them with blood curdling shrieks.

"The Iroquois will overtake those soldiers before they make it to the fort," I said.

"Give cover!" Captain Jansen shouted.

CHAPTER 7

HOLD FIRE!

Musket and rifle fire erupted along the parapet. I raised my musket and let off a shot. An enemy Indian darted behind the nearest tree and then fired back. I frowned. If I had my uncle's rifle, that Indian would not still be shooting at me. I let off another ball. It fell short and hit the ground.

Tracking Wolf and Jacob fired and reloaded beside me. Cannon boomed from an embrasure on the eastern wall.

The enemy Indians fell back, seeking cover in the tall grass and behind some brush. From there they sniped at the four men who lumbered toward the sally-port.

As they neared the fort, I saw the reason for their slow pace. Between them they carried a badly injured man. Blood dripped from his dangling, flopping and scalped head.[1]

"That must be the bateau man they couldn't find yesterday," Tracking Wolf said.

"Open the sally-port!" the captain shouted. "Get that poor man to the hospital."

Once on the parade ground, the soldiers lowered the injured man onto a litter. Congealed brains clung to the clotted blood that surrounded the hole in the back of his head. "That man will not live long," I said.

"At least he will die among friends who will mourn his loss," Jacob said. "That is good."

Beyond the fort the British Indians capered and shook their fists at us. They beat their chests and shrieked. They circled the fort, zigzagging from tree to bush as they moved closer.

I laughed at them. "Look at the prancing warriors!" I shouted. "See how they play at war?"

"Come closer!" Tracking Wolf yelled. "If you're so brave, come here and have a taste of our powder and shot."

"Pay no attention to the American dogs!" Joseph Brant shouted. "They question your bravery, but they hide themselves inside the enemy garrison." He sneered. "Before this siege ends, their fate will be sealed. In their time of famine, the Americans will happily eat their dogs!"

A chill shook me. The wolf of hunger nibbled at my innards. My throat tightened. I turned away from Brant and willed my ears to shut out his awful words. I jumped down from the parapet and ran to the water barrel. I drew in big gulps of water until I could drink no more. Only then did the panic and nausea go away.

The rest of the day inched along. All afternoon Brant's Indians sniped at us. A few British soldiers took shots at us as well. When any of them came too close, we opened fire and drove them back.

Suddenly, two Mohawks raced to a nearby field and grabbed bundles of our hay.

"Stop them before they set fire to the garrison!" I shouted. I fired at one of the Mohawks. He dropped the hay and grabbed his arm. He turned and ran back toward the British camp. The other Mohawk let go of his armload and took off running behind his wounded friend.

"Good shot," Tracking Wolf said.

"Hold fire!" Lieutenant Colonel Willett shouted.

Tracking Wolf lowered his musket. Occasional gunfire continued.

"Hold your fire!" Captain Jansen shouted.

An uneasy silence settled over us. A British officer dressed in an elaborately decorated red coat marched toward the fort.[2] Instead of a musket he held a flag – a white flag.

"Look!" Jacob whispered. "It's Gilbert Tice, the tavern keeper." He snorted. "The brave loyalist carries a cowardly flag."

Did the British intend to surrender? My heart beat a different rhythm, like a turtle rattle at a victory ceremony. My hope awakened and a longing for peace wrapped around me, warm and comforting like a beaver robe on a frosty morning.

At one side of Tice two officers in plainer dress uniforms kept stride. At his other side strutted two

Mohawk chiefs painted for war. The porcupine quill headdresses they wore on their roaches made them look fierce. They glanced up at us with arrogant eyes, as if to say, 'Now, brothers, you will pay for your foolishness.' Their mocking smiles showed me that it was not a British surrender they came to speak about.

I stood taller. I sneered at the Mohawks and raised my musket to show them my bravery.

The British officers' boots struck the ground hard as they approached the front gate.

I aimed my musket at Tice and his flag and wished again that I had Laughing Fox's rifle. Tracking Wolf pointed his weapon at one of the other officers. I glanced to my right. Every soldier on the parapet stood poised to shoot at the first sign of treachery, if the order came.

"Lower the drawbridge!" Colonel Willett shouted.

No! I wanted to yell. But I steadied my musket and stood ready to shoot in case the British or their

Mohawks rushed the fort. Time seemed to wait and see what would happen next.

My finger twitched on the trigger.

CHAPTER 8

FLAG OF TRUCE

Men rushed forward on the parade ground below. Chains clanked, ropes creaked, weights rumbled and lumber groaned as the heavy timbers of the drawbridge came down.

Two lines of Massachusetts soldiers formed on either side of the heavy doors. One company of the 3rd New York Regiment stood at the ready just beyond them. Could they hold off an enemy assault long enough for other soldiers to shut the doors?

"Send the man with your flag of truce forward!" Captain Jansen shouted to the British officers.

Gilbert Tice lifted the white flag higher as he approached the door. He held his body stiff, but his eyes darted here and there: sweeping the walls of the fort and then pausing to focus on the ring of sharpened sticks that encircled them. His glance lingered on each cannon, and on the American flag still fluttering from the pole. His eyes strayed to the Americans and Oneidas lining the parapet. He looked haughty, superior and disdainful, but the more he saw of the defenses and defenders of Fort Schuyler, the wider his eyes opened. Sweat glistened on his brow by the time the British drummer beat the Parley.

The fort's massive doors swung open. Our Continental fife and drum answered with the Cease Fire and Parley.

I took aim at one of the Mohawks in case he made a move to charge the open door. All along the parapet, soldier and Oneida alike stood at the ready.

"I am Captain Gilbert Tice of His Royal Majesty's Troops," he said as he strutted into the fort. "General St. Leger sends his greetings and an offer of mercy for you and your men."

The silence that answered him spoke more than any words could have. I wanted to turn and look down at the faces of the American soldiers in the fort, especially Gansevoort's, but I didn't dare let down my guard until the doors slammed shut and the locking device banged back into place.

"Halt!" Colonel Willett shouted at Tice. "We are prepared to receive your flag and your message. However, you must be blindfolded before you take another step."

"When you accept the Crown's offer and surrender Fort Stanwix, you will be allowed to leave here without fear of harm," Captain Tice said.

Silence answered him again.

"Apply the blindfold," Colonel Willett ordered.

A 3rd New York officer stepped forward. He held a folded white neckerchief taunt between his hands. Another soldier grabbed hold of Tice's shoulders and spun him around to face the doors. The officer placed the blindfold over Tice's eyes and yanked it tight before tying the knot.

"About face!" Colonel Willett said.

Captain Tice spun on his heel. A 3rd New York escort closed ranks on either side of him. "Forward march!" an officer shouted. The 3rd New York marched Tice away toward the barracks.

As the sound of tramping feet faded, I glanced up at the sky. The summer sun had slipped lower, but it would be hours before Skyholder darkened the sun and welcomed back the moon. I braced myself for a long wait.

At least these Americans wouldn't retreat from the power of the king's army as quickly as the soldiers at Ticonderoga had done. If we had to surrender Fort Schuyler, that decision wouldn't be made in haste.

I pulled in a deep breath of hot, sultry air. The pungent odors of trampled grass, hot sod and fermenting swampland caressed my nose. The heat and moist earthy scents lulled my senses. My head drooped. My eyes closed.

Startled, I jerked my head up and blinked the web of sleep from my eyes. The enemy escort still stood beyond the drawbridge under the blazing afternoon sun. Sweat stood out on the foreheads of the British officers; wet blotches ringed the collars and underarms of their woolen uniforms. They shifted their weight from one foot to the other as they waited. They kept their voices low so I couldn't hear what they said. Every now and then one or the other glanced toward the nearest tree as if he wished he could go there and recline in the shade.

After a while the two Mohawks squatted down on their haunches. One warrior poked the other's chest. That one scowled and picked up a stick. His eyes flashed with anger as he broke the stick into pieces. Suddenly he stood up and made a sign to the British officers. Both warriors ambled off toward the Indian encampment.

The British officers glanced over their shoulders, as if they feared the angry Mohawks might circle around and sneak up behind them.

So the British didn't dare to trust their Indians. Maybe the Mohawks and the other Loyalist Iroquois didn't trust the British either. Without trust an alliance could fall apart, like a sand hill in heavy rain. That might be good news for the Americans.

But what about our own alliance? Could we trust the Americans? Did they trust us? We had pledged to support their fight for liberty, what did they promise in return? I shrugged. Someday that would matter, but right now we had to fight together against the British. If we didn't, we would both lose this war.

I glanced down at the parade grounds. Captain Tice, blindfolded and surrounded by his Continental escort, marched back to the front gate.

"You have wasted valuable time with this feeble charade," Colonel Gansevoort said. At his signal the captain of the Massachusetts Company stepped forward and yanked the blindfold from Tice's eyes.

Gilbert Tice squinted at the sunlight. "Just remember," he said. "If you refuse to surrender this garrison, General St. Leger will use his superior force to execute the vengeance of the crown against you as willful outcasts."[1]

"You may tell your general that the American soldiers at Fort Schuyler are prepared to defend this garrison and our flag," Colonel Gansevoort said.

Tice flinched, as Gansevoort's words pelted his face like grapeshot. He drew himself up. "You will soon regret – "

"Open the gate!" Colonel Willett shouted.

The doors swung open. The 3rd New York marched Tice to the door. As soon as he stepped beyond the entry, the door slammed shut behind him and the locking device thumped into place.

"Raise the drawbridge!" Gansevoort shouted.

"Hold on!" Tice yelled. He broke into a run as the drawbridge began to rise. By the time he reached the end of the drawbridge, he had to jump. He hit the ground and stumbled forward. Laughter exploded all along the parapet when he landed face-first in the grass. He scrambled to his feet and swiped at the grass stains on his pants.

"You better go look for your fancy Indians," Private Jones shouted. "At least ours don't walk away when we need them."

"Outrageous!" a British officer yelled. "How can a civilized army negotiate surrender with such common people?"

I clenched my teeth. No wonder the Americans wanted to be free of these arrogant people. The British soldiers and their king treated us like we were no better than the dirt beneath their feet.

I threw my head back and gave a warbling war whoop. Tracking Wolf's voice joined with mine and blended with the answering calls of our pickets. For the first time, I felt at one with the American soldiers. For good or ill we would stand together to keep our common enemy at bay.

CHAPTER 9

BESIEGED

The next morning dawned, heralding another hot, sticky summer day. I searched the heavens for the clouds and colors usually sent by Skyholder before he hurled rain and flashing lights down to cool the sun's fire. I frowned at a cloudless blue dome above. There would be no escape from the sweltering heat today. I mounted the parapet at the northeast bastion as the first enemy shots rang out.

All morning Brant's Indians moved closer to the ramparts, darting from tree to bush. Some even took cover behind the potato plants in the garden. From their hiding places they recklessly dashed within range of our guns to snipe at anyone who dared to show themselves. At times, they fired so many rounds that we couldn't rise to return fire without risk of injury or death. The acrid odor of smoke from exploding gunpowder hung in the humid air.

"The bateaux guard won't be able to travel back to Fort Dayton today if the British keep this up," Tracking Wolf said as he joined me on the parapet.

"That's just as well," I said. "We'll need every man we have to hold back the British if they mount a direct attack."

"Private Jones says we have plenty of ammunition for muskets, but Colonel Gansevoort is holding back on cannon shot. He wants to be sure we'll have enough when we need it the most."

"Good," I said. "The British haven't thrown their full force against us, yet. So far they mostly wage war with their sharpshooters. When they do fire a field piece, the ball falls short and causes us no harm."

I rested my musket barrel on top of the parapet and ducked my head behind the bastion. I fired my musket blind in the direction of the enemy.

"There will be another raid tonight," Jacob said. "Sergeant Bailey says Gansevoort wants that barn and house that belonged to Mr. Roof burned.[1] He says they stand too close to the walls and give too much cover to the enemy."

Tracking Wolf grunted. "We will join them," he said.

I frowned at the heavy walls that caged me here. The thought of getting out on another raid gladdened my spirit. I longed to feel the rush of the chill night air against my bare skin, the prickle of danger along my scalp lock.

Evening shadows lengthened across the parade ground by the time we joined the soldiers preparing for the raid. Excitement pulsed in my blood with renewed strength and rhythm.

Private Jones straightened his blouse and settled his tricorn hat on his head. A smile creased his grimy face when he saw us coming. "You boys ready to help us torch Roof's place?" he asked.

I grunted and raised my fist high. "We are ready." I said. I stuffed one piece of dried venison into my mouth before I tossed my blanket and food pouch onto the pile of our belongings near the casemate wall. I chewed on the dried meat as I smeared black paint over my face.

I handed the paint jar to Tracking Wolf. "Hurry," I said. "Captain Jansen is already headed this way."

Tracking Wolf traced black lines across his blue face paint. "Good," he said. "That means we'll soon be underway." He sounded bored.

"Don't you want to go?" I asked in a low voice. I glanced over my shoulder, relieved to see Private Jones chatting with another soldier.

Tracking Wolf shrugged. "I'll go." He turned his face away. "I should tell you I'm thinking of joining the pickets outside the fort tomorrow. At least there I'll have a chance to prove myself in combat."

I bristled. "You don't think dodging balls and shot on the parapet takes valor? Aren't we proving our bravery by holding off the British day after day?" I snorted. "Who can deny our courage? We stand alone with the Americans against our former brethren who are poised to destroy us."

"I'm tired of the sameness," he said. He grinned. "I should have volunteered to carry messages like

Paul. Think of the excitement Paul must have felt – riding straight through the enemy lines like he did."

"Think of the danger," I said. "And consider the fate of this fort if all the Oneidas go off on foolhardy jaunts instead of staying here and standing firm."

The drummer beat the Assembly as Captain Jansen approached. The soldiers shifted into neat lines and stood straight, eyes forward.

The captain saluted. He inclined his head in our direction. "Before I go over the objectives for tonight's raid, I must ask for a few volunteers from our Oneida friends for a special mission."

The back of my neck tingled with unease. Surely he didn't expect us to volunteer without telling us what he wanted us to do? I glanced at Tracking Wolf and Jacob. They looked straight ahead. The other Oneidas behind us did the same. I cast my eyes down to the dry, dusty ground. Let someone else volunteer if they're crazy enough, I thought. It won't be Walks on Snow.

Tracking Wolf's elbow jammed into my ribs. I shot him an angry look and jumped forward to avoid his next blow. He stepped up beside me. Jacob moved up at my other side.

"Orderly!" Captain Jansen shouted. "Take these three men to Colonel Willett to be briefed on their mission."

What? I didn't volunteer for anything. I turned on my heel, determined to step back and rejoin the ranks.

Tracking Wolf grabbed my wrist and raised my arm high. "Huzzah!" shouted the American soldiers, applauding our willingness to serve.

The orderly waved his arm for us to follow. I aimed another foul look at Tracking Wolf and then fell in line behind the captain's servant. My blood still simmered with resentment when the orderly rapped on the door to Colonel Willett's quarters.

"Come!" the colonel ordered.

The orderly swung the door open. "Here are your Indians, sir," he said.

His Indians? I fumed. We didn't belong to this man or any white man!

Colonel Willett placed his quill in a stand and got up from his writing desk. He stood tall as he straightened his decorated blue uniform coat. His eyes probed mine, as if weighing my loyalty. Before his eyes moved on to Tracking Wolf, I saw his trust there.

My eyes lingered on his face. The curve of his nose, so like the beak of an eagle, comforted me. The eagle is the protector of the Oneidas, watching over us as our guardian and warning us of danger. I should not fear under this man's watchful eye.

I took note of his fancy, wooden spindle-back chair, his soft, curtained bed and the fine wooden cabinet in one corner of his room. Twilight glowed beyond his windowpanes and flickering candlelight danced across a neat, uncluttered floor. The last knot at the back of my neck loosened. This was a brave and worthy leader. Only an important warrior chief would have such a fine room and so many fancy furnishings.

"Thank you for volunteering to serve the American cause," Colonel Willett said. "Colonel Gansevoort has personally asked for your help."

I leaned forward, anxious to hear what he wanted us to do. Maybe he would ask us to bring a message to General Herkimer. My heart thumped as I imagined running with the wind at my back through the dark forest to Oriska. My father's pride and surprise, when he discovered that I had been chosen to carry an important war message to a chief American warrior, would be worth any dangers I might face.

Colonel Willett cleared his throat. "Your mission," he said, "is to infiltrate the enemy's camp and gather information vital to the defense of this garrison. Fort Schuyler must not fall into the hands of the British. The news you bring back will help us prepare for their next attack."[2]

My nostrils flared. He expected us to spy on the king's army?

I stared at Jacob and Tracking Wolf in shocked disbelief when they grunted agreement.

CHAPTER 10

THE MISSION

"Colonel Gansevoort depends heavily on your loyalty and your cleverness to complete this mission," Colonel Willett said. "He understands the danger you will face as you carry out these orders. He pledges his undying gratitude for your service. However, in the event that you are captured by the enemy, we will be unable to come to your rescue or to recognize you as agents of the American army."

My mind reeled with the awful possibilities. What if someone among the British Iroquois recognized us as rebel sympathizers? How could we explain our sudden change in loyalty? Would they believe us if we tried? What would the British and their Indians do to American spies? That's what they would call us. That's what we were, now.

I shuddered. Captured enemies were forced to run the gauntlet, and sometimes killed and scalped at the end. Spies endured worse treatment. Oneida spies would be tortured and slowly executed as traitors to our fellow Iroquois.

Colonel Willett offered me his hand. I gripped it, as if only he could pull me from the quicksand I had stumbled into.

"Godspeed," he said. His eyes looked weary as they locked with mine.

He's right, I thought, as the colonel shook hands with Tracking Wolf and Jacob. Only the Great Spirit is wise enough to help us now.

A few minutes later we loped through the sally-port. "What is our plan?" I asked. "Should we go our separate ways or stay together?"

Tracking Wolf's nervous laugh did nothing to reassure me. "Staying together may seem safer but that would be more dangerous, for us as well as for the mission."

"Especially for the mission," Jacob said. "If we

are caught together, no one will be left to bring information back to Gansevoort."

"What if someone recognizes us?" I said. "What will we say?"

Jacob folded his arms on his chest. "I'll say I'm fed up with the rebels and their war so I've decided to side with my fellow Iroquois and their British friends."

"I'm going to tell them that the words of the Mohawk, Joseph Brant, have convinced me to side with the British," Tracking Wolf said.

"Be careful about using Brant's name," I said. "They may ask him to verify your story and he is not easily fooled."

"What about you?" Jacob asked, as the guard pulled the sally-port door open.

"I guess I'll know what to say when the time comes," I said. I clasped each of their hands in mine. "May the Great Spirit watch over you until we meet back at the fort," I said.

"Let's make a promise," Tracking Wolf said. "If any one of us doesn't make it back to the fort, those who do will tell his true story to his father and mother. That way they will know about and honor his brave service."

"Agreed!" Jacob and I said together.

Tracking Wolf grinned. "And I will personally help Polly Cooper mourn her loss."

Before I had time to argue about that, he and Jacob raced out of the sally-port. I slipped out behind them. The guards at the redoubt trained their guns at the thick darkness beyond the fort. The quiet night hid any danger lurking ahead; a blanket of woolly clouds covered the young August moon.

I paused long enough to watch Jacob and Tracking Wolf lope away toward St. Leger's main encampment north of the fort. Then I turned and ran southeasterly, following the stream toward the Mohawk River and the British encampment there.

The night air, heavy with leftover humidity and evening dew, pressed down on me. When I reached the cleared land, I slowed to a walk. I stayed close to the brush and tall grasses along the banks of the stream.

I paused to watch Jacob and Tracking Wolf lope
toward St. Leger's main encampment . . .

Any minute I expected to be hailed by a British soldier or one of their Indians. I searched my mind for answers to the questions they would ask. If I told them the truth there might be someone among them who knew that my father, Eagle Tail, and my uncle, Laughing Fox, were working with the rebels at Oriska. That would make my claim of loyalty to the king suspect.

I rounded a bend of the creek and hunched down in the brush near the bank of the Mohawk River. The odor of wet, earthen banks mingled with the fishy smell of the water. The river burbled and surged between the banks. Mosquitoes hovered and hummed in my ears, but the bear grease I had rubbed on my skin kept them off me. Crickets chirped as I considered my options.

The campfires of the British flared and sputtered less than three hundred yards from where I squatted. The British and Indian sentries could be anywhere.

I wondered how Tracking Wolf and Jacob had fared. Had they managed to breach the enemy lines?

Did the British and their Indians believe their stories, or had their deception been exposed?

My throat tightened. Tracking Wolf and Jacob might already be in enemy hands. I might be the only one left to carry out the mission. I had to press on.

The sound of the rushing river hid any noise my moccasins made as I slipped from bush to tree. My lips twitched in a nervous smile as I approached the enemy camp with the speed of a turtle. My mother, Sweet Grass Weaver, daughter of the Turtle Clan Mother, would be pleased that I looked to the turtle for strength, patience and endurance.[1]

"Halt and identify yourself!"

I stopped and peered into the darkness. Rustling grass signaled the approach of more than one pair of moccasins.

I stiffened and fought an overwhelming urge to escape: to run headlong back to the fort, or race across the clear land and lose myself forever in the cedar swamp, or throw myself into the waters of the Mohawk and swim all the way to Albany.

I stood my ground and stole a quick glance back toward the fort. Flames danced where Roof's barn had stood.

Strong hands grabbed my arms from behind. At the same time a torch flared, so close to my face that the heat singed my forehead. I stared into the painted faces of two Mohawk warriors.

"Oneida!" one said, spitting out the word like a wad of rotten meat. Two sets of cruel eyes drilled into mine, probing and suspicious.

CHAPTER 11

AMONG THE ENEMY

"Tell us your name and the name of your village," one of the Mohawk warriors said.

I held my body taut, expecting the warrior behind me to strike the first blow with his tomahawk. I willed my knees to stand firm. "I am Hungry Bear," I said. "I have come here from my village at Oquaga to serve the king."

His eyes narrowed. "How do I know you tell the truth? For all I know you serve the Americans and have been sent here to spy on us."

Fear clutched my throat. The enemy behind me tightened his grip on my arms. I searched my mind for something they might believe.

"I am kin to Old Isaac, father of Joseph Brant's wife," I lied. "Chief Brant comes to our village often to visit his family. He told us that the king wants all Oneidas to strengthen the Iroquois Covenant Chain instead of crushing it by choosing to fight on the side of the Americans."[1] I lifted my head and looked my chief captor in the eye. "I have thought long about that. That's why I came here, to serve the English with my Iroquois brothers."

My chief captor nodded to the warrior behind me. When he let go of my arms, I let loose of my breath and rubbed my hands together to stop the prickling.

"I am Fighting Dog," my chief captor said. He studied me. "We will take you to our camp. You will tell us everything you have seen on your way here from Oquaga."

I stumbled after them; led by the two Mohawks I had seen and followed by the one behind. My mind reeled. They wanted me to prove my loyalty by giving up information about the Americans and my fellow Oneidas. At least I hadn't told them the truth – that I had come here from Fort Schuyler.

"I saw very little of interest as I traveled," I said. "I followed the Susquehanna River to the Unadilla and then struck out toward Old Oneida and Kanonwalohale.[2] I have heard that the Oneidas who live in those villages are allies of the Americans, so I kept to the woods and stayed clear of them. I didn't talk to anyone for fear they would attack me if they learned of my loyalty to the king."

The campfires of the enemy camp flickered up ahead. "Then what do you bring as an offering to the king?" Fighting Dog asked as we passed the sentry post.

The mingled aromas of simmering stew, boiled corn bread and roasted beef teased my hunger as we neared the campfire. My stomach growled and groaned. "I am prepared to offer the king whatever service he desires of me," I said, trying to keep my mind off my hunger so I could focus on my mission.

The Indian who walked behind me stepped up to the cooking pot. My heart faltered when I saw his Oneida headdress. Did he come from Oquaga? Did he know I lied?

"You must be hungry for hot food after your long journey," he said. He ladled stew into a bowl and handed it to me.

I searched his face for signs of treachery. He stared at something over my head. Why wouldn't he look at me? Did he know the truth and despise me for it?

I turned away before he could see the bowl shake in my hands. I drew in a deep breath. My mouth watered when I looked into my bowl. I sipped at the scalding hot broth and then pulled out a hunk of beef. I closed my eyes as the juicy meat fell apart in my mouth without even chewing. I grunted in satisfaction and sat down near the cooking pot.

The two Mohawks sat on their haunches off to my side, watching me. Distrust flickered in Fighting Dog's eyes. He leaned close to the other Mohawk and said something I couldn't hear. That Indian looked hard at me. He sneered and nodded.

The cooking fire flared. Flames licked at the green wood. Sap, the wood's life blood, hissed and popped as it bubbled up and then leaped into the fire. I sucked another piece of meat from the broth and swallowed it whole before the lump of fear closed my throat.

"I know this Indian, Howling Wolf," the Oneida said.

My heart sank to my stomach. I stared into the crackling fire, hoping this wouldn't be my last meal.

Fighting Dog and Howling Wolf got to their feet. "What do you know of him, Daniel?" Fighting Dog asked.

I tried to swallow but my tongue fell back in my throat and refused to move.

"I know his father, Many Beavers," Daniel said. "Hungry Bear is telling the truth. Like his father, he will fight for the king."

I stared into my empty bowl. I didn't dare to show them the surprise on my face or they would know that Daniel didn't speak the truth. Why did he lie for me?

I stood up and bent over the steaming pot. I ordered my racing thoughts to stop. I composed my face as I scooped up another helping of stew. "I wondered when you would recognize me, Daniel," I said. I turned to face him. "My father sends greetings to you and your family."

He didn't meet my eyes. "We are not here to gossip like women," he said. "We are here to help the king take the American fort." He turned and ambled toward the tents.

"You will soon have a chance to prove your loyalty to us," Fighting Dog said. "At sunrise tomorrow we mount a full-scale attack on the Americans." His harsh laughter chilled my bones. "You can show your love for the king by killing many rebels."

"Long live the king," I said. I raised my musket high above my head, eager to show my desire to join them.

Howling Wolf looked suspicious. "This is not the time to play at war," he said. "Get some sleep. Morning will come soon." He threw a blanket on the ground by my feet.

I wrapped the blanket around my shoulders and lay down with my back to the fire. I closed my eyes, but sleep refused to come.

Had Tracking Wolf and Jacob succeeded in convincing the British and Indians in St. Leger's army of their loyalty? If so, they might be on their way back to the fort by now with information about British troop strength. Perhaps they also had information about the plan to overpower the Americans in the morning. But what if they had failed?

I stared into the shadows. The encampment rumbled with snores. My eyes burned, begging for sleep. The fire slowly faded to glowing embers.

Colonel Gansevoort had to be told about the enemy plan to launch a full attack tomorrow.

I rolled onto my back. For just a heartbeat, Howling Wolf stopped snoring. I froze. I felt his eyes staring at me. My scalp prickled. I faked a snore.

I would have to wait until morning. Maybe then I could find out even more about their plans. Once the attack started, I might have a better chance to get away.

Polly's face floated in the wispy smoke from the warm coals. What would she think of me if she knew I had fallen into this web of deceit and deception? Would she sing of my valor, or refuse to hear my name ever spoken again? To my surprise I realized how much the answer to that question mattered.

The pale moon faded. A fiery light lit up the sky at sunrise, warning of an approaching storm.

Grunts and groans resounded as Indians and soldiers stirred and readied themselves for the day.

I struggled to my feet and rolled up my blanket. I stirred the coals from last night's fire. A handful of dry grass and a puff of breath brought the flames to life again. I added a few twigs and then went in search of bigger branches. The thought of another warm meal comforted me. I smiled to myself. I might die in battle today, but at least I wouldn't be eaten by the wolf of starvation.

"Prepare yourself for war," Daniel said, as he came up behind me. "There will be plenty of time to eat after the battle is won."

Reluctantly, I turned away from the tempting remains in the cooking pot. I grabbed my musket and loped after him.

As we neared Fort Schuyler, scattered shots from the rifles of Indian sharpshooters splintered the early morning quiet. Soldiers on the parapet returned fire.

I took cover behind a bush. My hands shook as I raised my musket and took aim at an American soldier.

My eyes blurred. If I didn't shoot, I would be shot by the enemy as a traitor. But how could I shoot the people I had pledged to help?

CHAPTER 12

THE KING'S BATTLE

An American soldier stood tall by the sentry box. I wanted to shout, 'Get down!'

A sudden puff of smoke marked the sharpshooter's shot. The soldier pitched back, likely dead before he hit the ground. Another man took his place. The next sharpshooter's bullet pierced that soldier's arm. Blood spurted between his fingers when he grabbed his wound.

"Get that man to the hospital," Captain Jansen shouted. "Sergeant Bailey, take his place!"

I shook my head. At this rate the Americans would run out of soldiers long before they ran out of ammunition.

Enemy musket balls thudded against the fort's walls and sprayed the parapet. But, while the sharpshooters focused on picking off the Americans, our Oneida pickets had time to regroup. Now they fired back at the sharpshooters. With their help, Sergeant Bailey might live to fight another day.

I looked behind me as Fighting Dog fired his musket at an Oneida picket. Had he noticed that I hadn't even fired a shot yet?

I raised my musket and pulled back the cock, but my hand shook so badly that I couldn't pull the trigger. Tracking Wolf and Jacob might have made it back to the fort by now. For all I knew they could be up there on the parapet. I lowered my musket. How could I risk killing my best friends?

"Shoot!" Daniel yelled as he ran toward me.

I swallowed hard and raised my musket.

"Shoot high," Daniel hissed in my ear. "But not so high it will be noticed." He raised his musket and took aim at an American soldier.

"I don't understand –"

I flinched when his gun went off, but the soldier didn't shriek or fall to the ground.

Daniel threw back his head and gave a long, wavering cry of victory.

I whooped with him and then took high aim at Sergeant Bailey. When I pulled the trigger, the sergeant didn't fall. I gave voice to my own triumph.

I sent a silent prayer of gratitude to the Great Spirit for sending Daniel to me. I still didn't know what he was up to, but for the moment he seemed to be on my side.

The rest of the morning passed by in a blur of gunfire, smoke and suffocating heat. The blazing sun glinted off musket and cannon alike, making it more difficult to focus on any target.

The British soldiers wilted in their heavy clothes. Sweat trickled down their red faces and stained their fancy jackets.

Around midday Daniel and I reclined under an old oak a short distance from the battle. The hottest part of the day would come later, but here in the cool shade a light breeze refreshed our bare skin above and below our breechclouts.

I wanted to ask Daniel why he didn't kill Americans, but when I opened my mouth he gave me an angry look and turned his back.

Exhaustion tugged at my eyelids. It was about this same time that warm day last fall when Tracking Wolf and I stopped to rest. We had been hunting deer all morning until the heat of the midday sun bore down on us. The scent of marshy earth led us to the bank of a stream. We drank our fill of the cold, clear water, and then reclined nearby in the shade. Dappled by muted sunshine, we discussed the tracks of the large buck we had seen in the soft mud beside the stream. We bragged that we would follow his trail later and bring him down with a single shot. When we got back home, all eyes would fall on us, every ear would yearn to hear how we took the biggest buck any warrior had ever taken in Kanonwalohale. A buck so large it would take all the women in our village to bring the carcass home from our hunting place. That deer would yield enough meat to fill every hungry stomach, and a hide large enough to make a new dress and moccasins for my mother, Sweet Grass Weaver. Her eyes would light with pride when she saw that magnificent hide. Her smile would widen as she talked about the elaborate quill and bead work she would fashion to decorate her dress.

Later, we would feast and celebrate the hunt. I smelled the succulent haunch roasting over the fire and heard the tasty juices spit at the flames that licked and sizzled its meat. Polly smiled at me as she stirred the cooking pot where big slabs of deer flesh simmered with dried leeks and corn. My stomach rumbled.

A sudden sharp pain in my shoulder forced my eyes open. For one heartbeat I didn't remember where I was.

Daniel gave my shoulder another kick. "Get up!" he shouted. "Lieutenant Bird is readying a British detail to burn the new barracks at the fort."

"What?" I said. I scrambled to my feet and picked up my musket. "What are we to do?"

"Give cover," he said as he trotted toward camp.

I raced to catch up. "Will they strike tonight after dark?"

Daniel scowled. "The lieutenant will talk to his Regiment of Foot Soldiers," he said. "He will tell us about his plan when he's ready."

I glanced back toward the fort and wished I had some way to warn them. Not that those fancy barracks would be missed by the Americans. I had heard Captain Jansen curse the crazy Frenchman who wasted precious time and money building them instead of completing the northeast bastion.[1]

As I loped into camp behind Daniel, the muffled sounds of musket and cannon fire floated to us from the fort on a hot breeze laden with black powder.

Daniel stopped and whirled to face me. "You must fight alone, now," he said. He looked away. "Many eyes will be upon you."

Before I could thank him, he sprinted toward the main British camp. Uniformed soldiers milled about there, rushing in and out of the officer tents and then hurrying back toward the fort.

The Indian camp looked deserted. Most of the warriors must still be fighting the Americans. A few sickly Indians reclined in tents or under trees. I wandered over to a slack-faced young Seneca who sat propped against the trunk of a maple.

"Will you be well enough to take part in the raid tonight?" I asked.

He squinted up at me through half-lidded eyes. "Do I look well enough?" he said. He opened his eyes wider and studied me. "I don't remember seeing you in camp."

"I am Hungry Bear," I said. "I came late last night from Oquaga to fight with Brant and his Mohawks."

He chewed on my words like he sought satisfaction from them. He swallowed hard. "I am Red Jacket," he said. "I came with Cornplanter to fight in Butler's army. It won't matter if I'm not well enough to fight tonight. Butler will have plenty more Indians to do his work."

He grimaced, groaned and grabbed at his swollen belly. He lurched to his feet and stumbled behind the tree to relieve himself. He grunted once or twice. The sharp odor of loose bowels tainted the air.

I wrinkled my nose. It was good that he had the freedom to empty his bowels outside where the fresh air could scatter the stink. At the fort we had been ordered to use the smelly necessary house in order to keep the garrison clean and healthy for the soldiers. I shook my head. How that disgusting stench could make Fort Schuyler a cleaner place I would never understand.

Red Jacket staggered back around the tree and fell to his knees. Sweat stood out on his forehead and upper lip.

I studied his face. Did he trust me enough to tell me what I needed to know about the British Indians? I quieted my racing heart while I waited for his labored breaths to slow.

"You say Butler has many Indians," I said, keeping my voice even. "I myself saw Oneida, Seneca and Mohawk warriors in the battle this morning."

Red Jacket snorted. "Didn't you see Cayuga, Onondaga and Delaware? If not, you still have much to learn. Didn't your ohwachira teach you anything?"

I hung my head. "There were so many warriors running about in the smoke, it was hard for me to tell one from another." I looked up. "How many fighting Indians does Butler have?"

He fixed wary eyes on me. "Some say about eight hundred." He gave me a sly look. "Maybe more." [2]

I smiled and pointed to my chest. "And one Oneida from Oquaga," I said.

His laughter erased the wrinkles from his young face. "Fight well for the king!" he called as I trotted away toward the British camp.

That Seneca was so eager to brag about the British Indian's great strength he was easy to deceive. I should have been proud, but guilt stabbed my heart and blackened my soul. I had betrayed the trust of my Iroquois brother and, worse yet, I had tricked him into helping his sworn enemy – me.

I shrugged off my shame as I drew nearer to the British camp. After all, I had only done what I had to do to protect the Americans and my fellow Oneidas. I didn't owe any allegiance to Indians who had chosen to stand against us with the king.

Fighting Dog stepped out from behind a gnarled hemlock tree. Porcupine quills enhanced his oiled scalp lock and decorated his gorget.[3]

Startled, I halted.

"Where have you been?" he said. He tightened his grip on his tomahawk, ready to use it on me if I gave the wrong answer.

CHAPTER 13

ATTACK!

"I just came from the fight at the fort," I said, forcing my eyes to hold his. "I heard the British were planning a raid so I came back to find out how I could help."

Fighting Dog took his hand off his tomahawk. "I will go with you."

I nodded. What else could I do? There would be no chance to escape for now.

Stifling heat rose up from the earth to meet the scorching rays of the afternoon sun as we headed for the British camp. I searched the heavens for some sign of rain, but found none. As we entered the camp my skin rippled with a sense of danger.

Behind Lieutenant Bird's tent one of the British officers held council with some soldiers. I followed

Fighting Dog to the place beyond Bird's tent where a group of Indians had gathered. I scanned their faces as we approached. Daniel was not among them.

"Hungry Bear wishes to join us," Fighting Dog said, pointing at me.

Howling Wolf scowled. "I thought you had gone back to empty the cooking pot," he said.

I gritted my teeth. Hunger gnawed at my stomach. I could have eaten ten beaver tails.

"There will be plenty of time to eat when the battle is won," I said.

Howling Wolf snorted. "I saw you gobble your stew and go back for more last night. Your desire for food makes you weak. A true warrior fights best when his belly is empty."

I grunted agreement and held my tongue. I had to convince him of my loyalty to the king, even if that meant swallowing my anger on an empty stomach. I wanted to tell him that someday we would meet face-to-face on another field of battle.

And when we did, he would quickly learn of my strength and courage.

Joseph Brant strode out of Bird's tent and headed our way. Fear shook my resolve. What if he recognized me from our brief encounter a few days ago in the woods outside the fort? I silently asked the Creator to cloud his vision so he wouldn't know me.

Joseph Brant stood tall and arrogant before us. I held my breath as I waited for his eyes to widen, and then flash with anger as he remembered where he had seen me. But his eyes flicked over me and moved on to Fighting Dog. I offered my gratitude to the Great Spirit and let go of my breath.

Brant stroked the blood-red vest that lay over his creamy, white linen shirt like the death flow that stains the neck of a fresh kill. "Today we will show the rebels at the fort and their traitorous Indians our full strength," Brant said. "They will then know the folly of their ways. We will punish them like the stubborn children they are. Before this day ends they will beg to surrender to their king."

I added my voice to the war-like grunts and cries of the others.

"Later we will feast and drink the king's rum," he said. "You will dance in honor of your courage in battle and tell of all your brave feats. Then we will return to our homes and await the king's rich reward for our service."

I raised my musket and gave a wavering whoop, but my insides trembled. Could Brant be right about the Americans surrendering? Did he have good reason to believe that they would? Or was he just lying in order to make these Indians eager to do his bidding?

"St. Leger will send a detail of soldiers to burn the barracks outside the wall of the fort," Brant said. "The Americans will be helpless to stop them because we will attack them at the same time. When they see how easily we kill them and destroy their buildings, they will give up this foolish fight."

I wished I could find some way to sneak back to the fort and tell Colonel Willett what I had learned.

But all I could do for now was to load my musket and fall into place behind Howling Wolf.

The hot sun slipped lower as we trotted along the Mohawk River toward the fort. We reached the upper landing and began firing as we advanced closer. We kept out of reach of the guns in the redoubt at the sally-port. We rounded the southeast bastion and headed toward the northeast bastion.

The British, led by Lieutenant Bird, sallied forth from the main camp and ran toward the new barracks.

"Attack!" Joseph Brant shouted. "Kill the rebels and take back this fort for the king!"

The fire of war burned hot in my blood. I raced forward, caught up in a surging swarm of Iroquois warriors. The patriot's musket balls rained down all around us. Cannon shot struck the ground as we ran, showering us with shredded earth and grass. I aimed high and fired at a soldier on the parapet. A musket ball whizzed past my head. I forced myself to keep moving forward, when all I wanted to do was turn and run for cover.

Howling Wolf charged ahead of me. His next shot pitched an American soldier off the parapet. His eyes glittered as he shrieked a hideous cry. "I claim that man's scalp after the surrender!" he yelled.

Stifling heat bore down on soldier and Indian alike. It lay on my chest like a slab of rock, so smothering I couldn't draw a deep breath.

"Fire!" an American sentry yelled. "They've set the new barracks ablaze!"

Flames snaked up the walls of the new barracks and twined through the roof timbers, like grapevines climbing to the sun. Thick, black smoke rose up from the inferno and rolled toward the north wall of the fort. As the fire intensified, choking smoke billowed over the parapet.

Searing heat scalded my face and hands. I peered through the smoke. As far as I could see, I stood alone now. The other Indians must have fallen back to focus their assault on the parapet above the sally-port.

Suddenly, the roof of the new barracks caved in, releasing a shower of flame, sparks and more blinding smoke. In the distance, the cheers of the British resounded. I coughed and choked as the thick, black fog of smoke wrapped around me.

Panic urged me to run from the smoke and flames before it was too late. I turned toward the British shouts and musket fire. But all I could see was a solid wall of smoke.

I paused. If I couldn't see them, how could they see me? This could be my chance to get back to the fort.

I bent low to the ground and took a deep breath. Without hesitation I covered my mouth and nose with my hand and plunged deeper into the smoke, toward the fire.

CHAPTER 14

ESCAPE

Unable to see, I dropped to my hands and knees and crawled. I struggled against the fear of being trapped by the flames as I crawled behind the burning barracks. This time my uncle wouldn't be here to help me get out.

The hot air burned my throat and nose as I rolled into the trench between the burning barracks and the north wall of the fort. Enemy musket fire seemed more distant here. So did the shouts and ferocious cries of the Indians. Smoke lay over me like a blanket.

No one will find me here, I thought as I burrowed under the musty hay in the trench. In the morning I will find some way to get back inside the fort.

I closed my eyes, but the crackling flames and hissing dew-wet grass outside the trench harried me. What if the drier grass near the ground caught fire? Would that blaze travel to me, ignite my covering of hay and burn me alive? My eyes snapped open. I held my breath and listened for the sound of approaching flames. Instead, a shrieking, undulating, terrifying whoop split the air.

My scalp prickled. Another voice joined the first, followed by another and another. The British Indians must have used the cover of the smoke to encircle Fort Schuyler so they could intimidate and threaten the Americans.[1] Would they dare to come close enough to discover my hiding place? I tensed, waiting for the sound of a tell-tale footfall to let me know they were near.

After what seemed like hours, I peered out from between the stalks of hay. A black sky loomed above me. The only light came from the charred remains of the new barracks that still smoldered and flared. I couldn't tell if it was smoke or clouds that hid the moon and stars. I had no way of knowing how long I had been hiding here or how long it would be before sunrise. Somehow I had to get closer to the fort before daybreak.

I rolled up out of the trench and scattered the hay over my hiding place. I dropped onto my belly pulled myself in the direction where the fort should be.

Yesterday's heat still waterlogged the air, making it hard to draw a breath. My hair, skin and breechclout reeked with the sharp smell of smoke. I licked my cracked lips with a swollen tongue. My throat ached for moisture. A sudden, sharp pain stabbed my belly.

I grabbed a handful of grass and chewed the tough stems and leaves hungrily. The dew on the blades moistened and soothed my tongue. But as soon as I choked it down, my stomach heaved the slimy mass back up and shot it out of my mouth. I pressed my face against the earth to smother the sounds of retching. Yellow wolf eyes laughed at me from the dark side of my mind. I gasped a breath and rolled behind a bush.

I searched the sky for a sign of first light. There, a rosy glow on the eastern rim of Mother Earth. As the blood-red sun slowly lifted, a shadowy outline of the sally-port redoubt appeared.

I staggered to my feet. Suddenly an Oneida warrior ran out from the sally-port and headed toward me. I dropped to the ground and rolled under the fraise, hoping he hadn't seen me. My muscles tensed, prepared to run away or fight.

I waited for him to get closer. In the time it took to take two breaths I heard his moccasins approaching my hiding place.

The grass under the fraise rustled as I raised my head to get a better look.

Daniel halted. He raised his tomahawk. "Show yourself," he said.

I froze, still as a totem. My mind raced. What was Daniel doing in the fort? Gathering information for St. Leger, or bringing information to Gansevoort? In either case he held the upper hand. I crawled out from under the fraise and stood to face him.

Daniel looked surprised. He lowered his tomahawk, and then without warning he tackled me. When we hit the ground he rolled us both under the fraise before he let me go.

"Colonel Willett expected you back long before now," he said. "He feared you might have been taken prisoner or killed."

Did he speak the truth? Or was he lying to trick me into admitting my allegiance to the Americans?

"I don't know what you mean," I said.

He looked annoyed. "I thought you knew, Walks on Snow. Why else would I lie to those Mohawks to save your skin? Why else would I show you how to shoot without killing Americans or our brother Oneida?"

I hung my head. "You're an American spy, too."

Daniel nodded. He looked toward the British lines. "Something big is happening in the enemy camp," he said. "An American sentry spotted a large group of Iroquois leaving just after sunrise this morning. I myself saw them heading southeast toward the landings." [2]

"Why would they leave?"

"St. Leger must have some other devil's work for them to do. I'm on my way back to the British camp to find out what they're up to."

"Maybe they're abandoning the siege. Perhaps they no longer think it's worth their while to take this fort."

Daniel grunted. "Or maybe they're planning to stop General Herkimer and his men from coming here to help us."

My heart fell into my empty stomach. "My father and uncle have gone to join General Herkimer," I said. "Someone should be sent to warn them."

"As soon as I learn the truth I'll get word back to Gansevoort," Daniel said. "Until then we can't be sure of their plan. As you said, they may have decided to go around Fort Schuyler and take their war to Albany instead."

"But what if you're right about their blocking Herkimer and his army? If that's true, it may be too late to warn them by the time you know that for sure."

"As far as we know, St. Leger isn't even aware that Herkimer is on his way to reinforce the garrison." Daniel gave me a stern look. "Anyone caught running off to warn Herkimer could alert the enemy to his approach. That would put Herkimer and all those who are coming with him in great peril."

I swallowed hard. "I understand."

"Do not tell anyone at the fort about my suspicions. There may be others who won't understand the need for more information before we act."

I nodded. "I'll keep your words to myself and I will ask the Great Spirit to bring you back to the fort soon."

Daniel grasped my hand before he rolled out from under the fraise. By the time I crawled out, he had already disappeared beyond the remains of the new barracks.

I set out for the sally-port, keeping close to the fort's thick walls. With any luck the British Indian sharpshooters wouldn't spot me before the Americans did. Occasional enemy musket fire greeted me as I neared the redoubt.

Why didn't the British mount an attack? By this time yesterday we already had the fort under full assault. Maybe their soldiers and Indians really were pulling out and heading for Albany. I wanted to believe that.

One of the soldiers at the redoubt pointed his musket at me. I halted. I dropped to a squat and held out my empty hands, hoping that the American soldiers wouldn't shoot an unarmed man.

CHAPTER 15

STORM WARNING

"Hold fire!" Private Jones shouted from the parapet. "That's one of our Indians."

The soldier at the redoubt lowered his musket. "Open the sally-port!" he shouted.

I scrambled to my feet and raised my hand in thanks to Private Jones. When the door swung open, I bolted into the sally-port.

"Walks on Snow!" Sergeant Bailey shouted from the parade ground. "Colonel Willett is waiting for your report. You are to come with me."

I stumbled after him, eager to give my report and then get something to eat and drink.

A short time later I left the colonel's quarters and made my way to the parade ground.

"Walks on Snow," Tracking Wolf called. "Jacob and I got back late last night. What took you so long?"

Jacob grabbed me by my shoulders. "I told Tracking Wolf you probably deserted to the enemy when you saw all the food they had."

His words stung. My legs shook, weakened by lack of sleep and hunger. "I haven't taken food or water for many hours," I said.

Tracking Wolf pulled me toward the storehouse. "Your belly does look skinny," he said. "Didn't the British feed you at all?"

I scowled and grunted. As soon as we reached the storehouse I devoured two hunks of bread without chewing and reached for more.

"Slow down," Tracking Wolf said. "Too much food on an empty stomach will not stay down long."

I carefully ground the next piece of bread between my back teeth. Then I chewed on a piece of dried venison. My stomach gurgled and growled, but it willingly accepted my food offerings.

We walked in silence to the water barrel. The fort's foul water wet my parched tongue and quenched my thirst. The British had dammed up the stream so the sally-port spring had gone dry. The chunk, chunk, of shovel thrusts signaled the digging of another well.

"Look out!" I yelled, yanking Tracking Wolf back as a bomb from a British mortar exploded on the parade ground.

Tracking Wolf laughed and brushed my hand away. "Don't worry," he said. "British bombs are like little apples young children throw over a fence."[1]

Jacob raised his eyebrows. "I saw you flinch, Tracking Wolf," he said. "Are you afraid of apples?"

I grinned. For once I wasn't the butt of Jacob's joke.

Tracking Wolf scowled. "I'm not afraid of the British or their flying shot," he said. He shook his tomahawk at the remains of the exploded shell to show his bravery. I laughed as he capered back up on the parapet and ducked down behind the sentry box.

I clambered up onto the parapet behind Jacob. An enemy musket ball pinged against the nearest cannon. I whooped and laughed. "Those red-coated Indians are so bold they think their muskets can kill our cannon," I said.

Jacob fired at the sharpshooter and then ducked for cover. "What do they have to fear?" he said. "They have a promise of protection from the king himself. He guarantees them great rewards for bringing the colonial rebels to their knees."

"They'll soon find big holes in the king's promises," Tracking Wolf said. "We have seen for ourselves how well he kept the promises his agent, William Johnson, made to us."

"Did you learn anything important on your mission?" Tracking Wolf asked.

I ached to tell him what Daniel had told me but I gave my word to keep his words to myself.

"No," I said. "But I did give Colonel Willett a fair tally of the number of British Indians."

I leaned closer. "What did you learn at St. Leger's camp? Does it look bad for the Americans?"

Tracking Wolf's eyes lit up. "They have plenty of soldiers there, many Royal Yorkers and Germans they call 'Jägers'. They have enough men to easily hold us in their snare. But they also know that we are well protected. They think it will not be easy to breach our defenses. Many of their soldiers are still trying to clear the felled trees from Wood Creek so they can move their supplies and heavy equipment into their camp."

"Many Indians and some whites are led by Brant, as we know," Jacob added. "But two Seneca warriors, Cornplanter and Old Smoke, were chosen by council to be War Captains of the British Indian forces. We also learned that Major Butler is on his way here from Three Rivers with another large group of Iroquois. They expected him to arrive by late afternoon yesterday."

"Did you hear anything that would explain why so many Indians left camp this morning?" I asked.

"No," Tracking Wolf said. "But that made the Americans uneasy."

I thought about my father and my uncle, on their way here with Herkimer and his militia by now. What if Daniel had been right? What if those enemy Indians had headed out to attack them?

I raised my eyes. Dark, puffy clouds to the east signaled an approaching storm. A hot breeze singed my face, the air already charged with the power of the lightning that would soon come.

CHAPTER 16

THE MESSAGE

"Look sharp!" Captain Jansen shouted. "Give cover to those militiamen running from yonder woods."

I fired at a Seneca warrior who was closing in on one of the men. He dropped his tomahawk, spun around and fell to the ground. The other pursuers slowed pace and then gave up the chase as a volley of balls rained down from the parapet.

Did I kill that Seneca? He lay still as death, sprawled on his back on the grass. My hands trembled. I had never killed a man before. He could be Red Jacket, the sick Indian left back at camp yesterday. That possibility wrenched my gut. I recalled how foolishly he had put his trust in me and that stained my spirit with regret. I groaned.

Whoever he was, that Seneca used to be my brother in the League of the Haudenosaunee.

I clenched my teeth to silence the moan of grief that rose up from my wounded heart. Bitter bile scalded my throat. I leaned over the parapet and vomited.

Tracking Wolf's strong hand gripped my shoulder. "You saved that American's life," he said. "These men have probably come from Herkimer's army. If they had been killed or taken prisoner, we would never know what message they carried."

I wiped my mouth with the back of my hand. "If they did come from General Herkimer, they may know something about the Oneidas who joined Herkimer at Oriska."

"Open the sally-port!" Captain Jansen shouted.

The first militiaman burst out of the sally-port as we reached the parade ground. Welts marked the insect bites on his grimy face and hands, and sweat stained his coat.

"I'm Lieutenant Adam Helmer," he said to the guard. He turned to the men behind him. "This is

Captain Marks Demuth, and Private Johan Yost Folts. We bring Colonel Gansevoort a letter from General Herkimer."

"Don't forget the cannon," Captain Demuth said. "General Herkimer requests that you fire three cannon as a signal that we made it to the fort."

"Prepare the cannon!" Colonel Willett shouted. "Fire three when ready!" He turned back to the militiamen. "Follow me to the officer's dining room," he said. "While you refresh yourselves I will see if Colonel Gansevoort will see you in his quarters."

Lieutenant Helmer's face reddened. He balled his hands into fists. "Good God, sir! There's no time. We were sent out yesterday but couldn't find our way past the British and their Indians until now. The General and our men must be almost here. They need your help now!"

"Take these men to my quarters," Colonel Willett said to his orderly. "I will alert Colonel Gansevoort immediately."

"Did you hear?" I asked Jacob. "General Herkimer is almost here."

"That means my father and mother will join us soon," Jacob said. "This siege will not last long when they get here."

Tracking Wolf whooped. "It will be the British who surrender when they see Hanyery and Two Kettles Together ride in with their guns smoking."

"And our other brave warriors," I said. "Don't forget about Thomas Spencer and his brother Edward, my father, Eagle Tail and my uncle, Laughing Fox –"

"And Blatcop, and my brother, Cornelius," Jacob said.

I looked to the east. The gathering storm darkened the sky. Black, billowing rain clouds marched from Oriska with Herkimer and his militia. A strengthening wind swirled across the cleared ground and beyond, tossing tree branches and leaves in its wake. I sniffed at the hot air, ripe with the scent of wildflower and gunpowder.

I scanned the fields and forests around us. Only occasional musket fire sounded from the enemy. Why? Because most of the British and their Indians had gone to meet Herkimer and his men as Daniel feared? If so, Herkimer's army and the Oneidas who came with them were in great danger. They had to be warned.

"I have to go," I said.

Tracking Wolf laughed. "Don't forget to use the necessary house," he called as I landed on the parade ground.

I faked a run toward the necessary house and then, keeping close to the walls, headed for the sally-port.

"Halt!" a Massachusetts soldier said.

I stopped and turned to face him. "I am an Oneida scout," I said. "I have an important message to bring to General Herkimer."

The soldier's eyes narrowed. "Colonel Willett sent me to find you," he said. "You are to come with me to his quarters immediately. He didn't say anything about sending you to Herkimer." He whirled and headed for Willett's quarters.

I jogged to catch up.

"Walks on Snow," Colonel Willett said, smiling and extending his hand as soon as the door swung open.

"This Indian says you told him to take a message to General Herkimer," my escort said.

Colonel Willett's eyes went cold, his smile disappeared. "That will be all, private," he said to the soldier.

The door closed. Colonel Willett turned away from me and stared out the window. "I never asked you to go to Herkimer," he said. He whirled to face me. "Who did?"

"No one," I said. "I just thought – "

"Who sent you to betray me? Bird? Brant?" He drove his fist into the wall. "Answer me!"

What could I say to make him believe me, now that I had lied and branded myself a traitor? 'Your word is your honor,' my father often said. I hung my head, ashamed that I had dishonored my father with my deception.

"I lied to that soldier," I said. "No one told me to go. I had reason to believe that Herkimer and those who will fight with him could be in great danger." I looked him in the eye. "I just wanted to warn them."

Colonel Willett held my eyes with his. "How can I be sure this is not another hoax?"

"I speak the truth, now," I said. "My father and uncle are with Herkimer's army." I turned toward the door. "I must go to them."

Colonel Willett stepped between me and the door. "It's already too late for that. I just received another message from Daniel. He tells me that Sir John Johnson and John Butler are leading the British troops and Indians to block Herkimer."

"I can outrun them," I said. "I will run faster than they can march."

Fatigue rimmed Colonel Willett's eyes. "I need you here," he said. "I'm preparing to lead a sortie out of the fort to provide a diversion. That's the only way we can help them." His eyes drilled into mine. "I need to send you out of the fort on a secret mission, one that can only be carried out by someone familiar with Lieutenant Bird's camp. Someone I can trust."

I held my head high. "I swear on my father's honor, I will not betray you."

Willett's stern eyes probed mine. I didn't blink or look away until I saw the tight muscles of his jaw loosen. "Your father stands with Herkimer," he said. "Will you stand with him?"

The scent of danger flared my nostrils. Pride and excitement pulsed in my blood. I raised my musket high. "I will!"

CHAPTER 17

WILLETT'S RAID

I slipped out the sally-port and bent low to the ground as I worked my way along the stockade to the southeast bastion. Once there, I scanned the ground between the fort and the river before I plunged into the tall grass. I darted through the meadow, flitting from bush to tree. My heart beat like a water drum as I approached the British camp.

I slipped off my moccasins and held them up to keep them dry as I slid down the near bank and waded into the Mohawk River. The reflection of my painted face rode the current as I caught a handful of water to quench my thirst.

A jagged flash of light in the darkening sky, a rumble of thunder and a sudden burst of wind urged me to get out of the water.

Responsibility hung around my neck, heavy as a millstone. If I failed to complete this mission, Colonel Willett would never trust me again. Worse yet, my father and uncle might die before this day ended.

I cringed. I would have to tell my mother it was my fault that my father and her brother died, and the families of all the other warriors who would fall with them. I hung my head. I would never be able to speak to Polly of that shame.

I lurched up the bank, slipped on my moccasins and sprinted away. I skirted the British camp and then circled back, hoping they might believe I had come from Oriska if I approached from the lower landing.

The spirit of the Evil Twin suddenly hurled one jagged spear of fire after another, each flash followed by a thunderous boom.[1] The power of his evil raised the hair on my scalp lock and surged around me. The fury of the storm strengthened. Rolling thunder shook the ground beneath my moccasins when I spotted the first British sentry.

"Halt!" an 8th Regiment officer shouted.

I skidded to a stop. "I am a runner from the battle," I said, panting. "I have an urgent message for Lieutenant Bird from Sir John."[2]

"Take this Indian to Lieutenant Bird," the officer said to an aide.

When we reached Bird's tent, I handed the false message to the aide. "Wait here," he said. He lifted the tent flap and disappeared inside.

Rain pattered the leaves above my head. Then, in the blink of an eye, the sky opened and a torrent of rain poured down on me.

Any minute I expected to be unmasked and seized by the British as an American spy. Colonel Willett had warned me that I would be listed as a deserter if I failed to return – a traitor to the American cause. I steeled myself to stand firm as I waited for rough hands to grab me from behind. In my mind they already knew that the message I brought them was false.

I looked over my shoulder, expecting to see soldiers running at me with their guns primed. But no one even looked my way. I raised my face to the sky and let the rain pound my face and cascade off my chin. When I looked down, muddy water swirled and puddled around my moccasins.

By the time the British foot soldier reappeared I had to clench my jaw to keep my rising panic from clacking my teeth together.

"You are to return at once to the battle with this message for Sir John Johnson," the soldier said. He pressed a folded piece of paper into my hand.

I glanced toward the Indian camp, wishing I had enough time to go and look for Red Jacket.

A British drummer beat Assembly. Soldiers ran out from their tents.

The foot soldier scowled. "Make haste!" he barked.

I turned and raced south toward Oriska. As soon as I could no longer see the camp behind me, I plunged into a stand of trees at the bend of the river and dove behind a log.

Would Bird swallow the bait? If he did, he would soon appear, on his way to help Johnson. But what if he knew that the message was only a trick to lure him out of camp? What if they had sent me away so they could lay in ambush, for Willett? I wrestled with those questions, but I couldn't find an answer.

Time passed slowly. After a while the rain let up. The odor of sodden earth and soaked wood scented the air. A cool breeze showered me with the leftover raindrops on the leaves overhead.

I held my breath and listened. If Willett's sortie had reached Bird's camp before the soldiers left, I should hear musket fire. If I didn't hear anything soon I would have to circle back and scout the encampment.

My shoulders slumped. Going back to the enemy would be more dangerous than before, especially if they had figured out where my loyalty lay.

Tramp! Tramp! Tramp!

My spirit soared at the approach of many marching feet. Bird must have believed my message. He was headed for the battlefield near

Oriska, leaving their camp defenseless against Willett and his men.

I peered out from behind the rotting log. Bird and a detachment of his 8th Regiment marched past at a brisk pace in tight formation. Red coats and metal buttons blazed beneath the clearing sky. The soldiers held their heads straight. Their eyes glittered, hardened for the task at hand.

I had never seen a more fearsome sight than that mass of British soldiers, marching off to make war. They held their backs ramrod straight and clamped their jaws with fierce determination. I waited until the last line of soldiers disappeared around a bend in the road before I dared to move.

Willett's sortie must be underway by now, I thought, as I trotted back along the road to the lower landing.

When I entered the Indian camp, musket fire erupted from the Royal Yorker's camp just beyond. I reached the British camp in time to see Sir John Johnson running for the riverbank with his wife and their guards.[3]

Stunned, I stopped. The message I brought to Lieutenant Bird said that Johnson was at Oriska. If Bird had realized that Johnson had already returned to camp, my ruse would have been discovered. By now I would be a British prisoner or, more likely, dead.

I thanked the Great Spirit for sparing my life and looked toward the river. Massachusetts soldiers and at least one Oneida scout chased after Johnson and his family.

"Check the perimeters!" Captain Jansen shouted. "This camp may not be abandoned. This could be a trap."

The 3rd New York Captain, Bleecker, stepped forward. "Fan out in all directions!" he shouted. He turned to me. "Scout yon woods! Report back to me any British or Indians you spy lurking there."

I trotted into the woods, my musket primed and ready. Sunlight and shadow played tricks with my eyes as I moved silently from tree to tree. My nerves tingled with a deadly mix of fear and excitement.

Suddenly a twig hit the ground near my feet. I whirled, raised my musket and scanned the tree limbs above for an enemy sniper.

A squirrel on a branch above my head scolded my poor eyesight.

I let out my breath and then plunged deeper into the woods. I scouted the forest in every direction, but nowhere did I find any sign of the British or their Indians.

I retraced my steps out of the woods and trotted over to Captain Bleecker. "I did not find any enemy soldiers or Indians in yon woods," I said.

"Well done," he said, looking distracted.

The American soldiers buzzed in and out of the British tents like bees at their nest. They carried out stacks of books, papers and letters and piled them up. Two Massachusetts men ran out from Johnson's tent with a British flag. Another man handed Bleecker the four camp colors he had pilfered from the camp's perimeter.[4]

"Look sharp!" Captain Bleecker shouted. "Throw anything too big to carry into the latrine!

Gather up the booty so we can get moving."

A New York soldier dumped an armload of fancy green uniform coats in the latrine.

I trotted over to Captain Jansen. "Where is Colonel Willett?" I asked.

"He's yonder with the advance forces," he said, pointing in the direction of the Indian camp.

As I sprinted toward the Indian camp, sporadic musket fire signaled the start of the American raid.

An Indian woman screamed. American soldiers set fire to the Indian shelters. Other Iroquois women herded their wailing children away from the fire and into the brush. Black smoke twisted up from the smoldering bark shelters, and from my heart. I struck my chest with my fist in despair.

Soldiers slashed the tents with their bayonets. They looted tents and shelters, some hauling out kettles, bolts of cloth, silver pieces and wampum, others grabbing blankets, guns and ammunition. Anything they didn't steal they smashed to pieces with their rifle butts. Pilfered hatchets split the rum and water barrels. The soldiers left them to pour out their contents in the dirt. One man cut down a deer carcass and dragged it through the dirt before he tossed it into a pit full of animal innards and human waste.

My stomach churned. Why did the American soldiers do this? These Indians would suffer enough when they saw what had been done to their things. Must they starve as well?

I raced back to the place where I had last seen Red Jacket. Two bodies lay crumpled near the tree. I stepped closer and peered down at the first one. Blood clotted on the breast of the Mohawk, Howling Wolf. He stared up at Skyholder's heavens with unseeing eyes. I turned to the other body.

I cringed when I saw his Oneida headdress. I stepped closer and looked down at his painted face. I staggered back, relieved that it wasn't Daniel.

Where was Red Jacket? Had he gone with Butler to head off the militia? Or had he died by my musket ball yesterday?

"Form up!" The 3rd New York Captain Van Benscouton shouted. "Repair to the rear for the return march to the fort!"

I fell in behind a New York division. I shook my head as we marched back along the path of destruction in the devastated camps.

The debt for this desecration would not go unpaid. Wounded British pride would fuel the fury of their next assault on Fort Schuyler. This humiliating raid on their camp would only increase their resolve to punish the rebels and bring them to their knees. As for the Iroquois, they would be infuriated by the destruction of their shelters and the theft of their belongings. I shuddered. Would they fault the Americans or the Oneidas for this despicable act?

The hot August sun dried the trampled grass near the road where we marched along the river. Locusts and crickets sang from hiding places in the tall grass. Mosquitoes circled my head and hummed in my ears. I brushed them away and listened for gunfire.

The only sounds were those made by the soldiers. They clomped along in their noisy boots and shoes. They laughed, shouted and groaned as they struggled under heavy loads of plunder. Anyone within a few hundred yards must know of our location.

My nostrils flared, trying to detect the smell of gunpowder, bear grease, sweat or any other scent of impending danger on the air.

"Walks on Snow!" Captain Jansen shouted.

I trotted to catch up with him.

"Advance to the front of the column and scout ahead," he said. "St. Leger will have heard about this raid by now. He may be setting a trap for us."

I sprinted ahead of the column and veered into the tall grass. I stopped and held my breath, listening.

A woodpecker hammered a half-dead tamarack blackened by last year's lightning strike. Birds surrounded me with song. They twittered among the branches overhead and uttered no startled cry of warning. But enemy Iroquois could be hidden behind any bush or tree, their quiet presence unknown to any other living thing.

I had to find out if the enemy lay hidden in ambush so I could warn Willett and his men. Danger clawed the back of my neck as I stole past a clump of brush. I clutched the handle of my tomahawk and slipped from tree to tree.

Suddenly, a hand grabbed my shoulder from behind. All the air left my body as I whirled to face my attacker.

CHAPTER 18

WILLETT'S SCOUT

I gulped a breath, raised my tomahawk and swung it at him. My opponent grunted. His muscular arm blocked my blow. Breathing hard, I grabbed hold of his oily wrist. I didn't dare look at him, afraid I wouldn't be able to strike a killing blow if I looked him in the eye. If I hesitated, he would kill me and my death would allow him and his brothers to slay many Americans. I gritted my teeth and aimed my hatchet at his forehead.

"Save your bloodletting for the enemy," Daniel hissed.

Stunned, I dropped my tomahawk. "I could have killed you," I said as I bent to retrieve it. "What are you doing here?"

A spark of humor flickered in his eyes. "Scouting for Colonel Willett," he said. He fears St. Leger's revenge for his raid."

I nodded. "Captain Jansen sent me out to do the same."

BOOM! BOOM!

"The Americans are firing cannon at the fort!" I shouted. I took off running, my body slicing through the grass like a scalping knife. Daniel loped beside me.

As we followed the branch of the Mohawk toward the fort, we spied some of St. Leger's soldiers. They must have circled around from the main camp so they could attack Willett and his men before he reached the fort. But they had strayed too close to the garrison's guns. American and Oneida muskets barked at them from the bastions.

Daniel and I ducked behind a tree.

The British soldiers moved into formation and returned fire at the fort. But when a barrage of musket balls spewed from the parapet, the cowardly redcoats ran for cover like scared rabbits.

American jeers and catcalls sailed out from the fort on the late afternoon breeze. More musket fire peppered the enemy. I laughed as the panicked British fled the field in complete disorder.[1]

Daniel leaned close. "I will tell Willett about this," he said. "You alert the fort of his approach." Before I could answer, he plunged back into the tall grass and disappeared.

Oneida pickets came out from the woods near the fort. I wanted to run to them, but I would have been listed as a deserter by now. A turn-coat wouldn't be welcomed back. A traitor would be shot!

I moved closer, slipping from bush to tree in order to circle behind the pickets. I peered out at them from behind a big white pine.

Tracking Wolf stood with his back to me, his musket raised. He seemed to be studying the land between the fort and the British encampment. I tossed a pebble at his back.

He whirled around. When he saw me, his eyes widened. His mouth dropped open.

I silenced him with my eyes and beckoned to him.

He frowned and aimed his musket at me. "I can't believe you dare to show your face here," he said.

"You don't understand —"

"You're right about that," Tracking Wolf said as he advanced on me. "You have brought shame to our Nation, and to your family and friends. When you turned against the Americans, you turned your back on all of us." He yanked my musket off my back and prodded me toward the fort.

"I must see Colonel Gansevoort," I said.

"You'll see him," Tracking Wolf said. "He personally ordered your capture. He wants you taken to his quarters."

As we made our way to the sally-port, other Oneida pickets joined us.

"Here is the traitor, Walks on Snow!" one of them shouted. He spit in my face.

I hung my head.

The guards at the redoubt trained their guns on me. My knees buckled. I stumbled. Two Oneidas grabbed my arms and hauled me upright. I closed my eyes. I couldn't bear to see the soldier pull the trigger.

"I bring this prisoner to Colonel Gansevoort as ordered," Tracking Wolf said.

I opened my eyes.

The soldiers lowered their guns. "Open the sally-port to receive a prisoner!" one of them shouted.

My escort propelled me through the sally-port and onto the parade ground. "I bring a prisoner for Colonel Gansevoort," Tracking Wolf said to Lieutenant Barns.

"Well done," Barns said. "Colonel Gansevoort will see to this man's punishment."

I searched the lieutenant's face for some sign that he knew the truth about me. He scowled and looked away. When he raised his hand, American soldiers stepped forward and surrounded me. One of them bound my wrists behind my back. They prodded me with their muskets as they marched me to the colonel's quarters.

Panic squeezed my heart. Gooseflesh stood up along my arms. Would Gansevoort continue this deception and have me shot or hung just to prove his lie?

A smothering blackness overshadowed my spirit and laid bare my soul. No one would ever speak again of my loyalty, or tell about my honor and my bravery. From now on I would be known as Walks on Snow, the Oneida who turned his back on his people and the cause of liberty. My father would never forgive me.

A soldier yanked the door to Gansevoort's quarters open. Rough hands shoved me inside; I stumbled and fell face-first on the floor.

Strong hands grabbed my arms and pulled me to my feet. "Here is the traitorous Indian," Lieutenant Barns said.

Colonel Gansevoort fixed his gaze on the space above my head. "Post a guard outside my door while I deal with this man," he said.

I held my back and head straight. If I had to die a traitor's death for my loyal service, at least I had one last chance to complete my mission. Whether he chose to disclose it or not, Colonel Gansevoort knew the truth.

My knees wobbled as I looked him in the eye. "Colonel Gansevoort," I said. "Colonel Willett sends word of his impending triumphant return."

Colonel Gansevoort blew out his breath. "Praise God," he said. He opened the door a crack. "Orderly!" he shouted. "Call the men to the parapet and send Lieutenant Barns to me at once."

From the parade ground a drummer beat Assembly.

Gansevoort turned to me. "Well done," he said. "Your service to this garrison has been invaluable to our cause."

My body sagged against the surge of relief that washed over me like a spring flood. I struggled to slow my racing heart and to contain my pride.

"Free this man's hands and make haste to clear his name," Colonel Gansevoort said to Lieutenant Barns when he arrived. "Let it be known that he secretly left this fort with my blessing to provide cover and support to Colonel Willett. He is not now, nor was he ever, a deserter. He has returned to us a hero after accomplishing a mission vital to Herkimer and his militia, and to the defense of this fort."

Too bad my father wasn't there to hear Colonel Gansevoort's praise. But at least my friends now knew that I had not betrayed them or the Americans. I held my head high and stuck out my chest as I strode out of the colonel's quarters.

"Walks on Snow," Tracking Wolf called as he ran to catch up with me. "I'm sorry I didn't give you a chance to explain why you left the fort." He looked embarrassed. "I should have known you would never be disloyal."

"I understood your caution," I said. "But I hoped you would help me get my message to Colonel Gansevoort." I snorted. "I guess in your own way you did do that."

Tracking Wolf grinned. "At least I didn't shoot you first and drag your lifeless body to Gansevoort's office."

I laughed. "You would have found yourself in big trouble if you had done that."

He laughed, too. "I can't wait to hear all about your mission," he said. "How did you get past Bird and his soldiers? Were you with Willett when he started his raid?"

There was something different in the way he clasped my shoulder, like I was an important war envoy now.

"I'll tell you everything in good time." I said as we reached the parapet. "Look! Here comes Willett and his men."

All along the parapet muskets rose, ready to protect Willett's sortie from a British ambush. I scanned the fields and woods. Not a redcoat in sight.

Willett led his victorious soldiers in through the sally-port. When they reached the parade ground, one soldier grabbed the stolen enemy colors and ran them up the flag pole. The British colors fluttered in defeat below the American flag. I raised my musket in salute.

"Huzzah!" every man on the parapet shouted. "Huzzah, Huzzah!"

Daniel strode out of the sally-port behind the soldiers. I ran down from the parapet and clasped his arm. "Was there any word of General Herkimer in the letters and papers taken from the British camp?"

Daniel looked grim. "I don't know what was in those papers," he said. "But one of the captives told me that a bloody battle was fought this morning near Oriska."

A cold chill stoked my dread. "What about Herkimer and his militia?"

He shook his head. "Most dead if that prisoner told the truth."

Most dead! Those awful words seared my soul. "What about the Oneidas who marched with them?"

His eyes reflected my sadness. "Many died, many others injured."

I closed my eyes and imagined the carnage, the bloody bodies of dead and wounded Americans and Oneidas scattered along the road.

I opened my eyes. "Did you hear anything about my father?" I asked, but Daniel had walked away.

Jacob ran up to me. "Did you hear about the ambush?" he asked. "Some say Herkimer and all his men have been killed or taken prisoner. One saw my father take a ball to his wrist."

'Most dead!' Daniel had said. His words still echoed in my mind. Grief wrapped itself around my soul, strangling my hope.

"I have to go, Jacob," I said. "My mother and my father's mother call me to the battlefield. I must go and search for them."

CHAPTER 19

MY FATHER CALLED MY NAME

I trotted toward the barracks to ready myself for the run.

"Jacob told me you were going," Tracking Wolf said when he caught up. He darted in front of me, forcing me to halt. "I will come with you. But we have a duty to the Americans first."

"What about my duty to my family?" I pushed him aside and ran on.

He reappeared, loping beside me. "What will Eagle Tail think of you if you abandon the Americans in their time of greatest need?"

My resolve wavered. My feet slowed.

"Didn't Laughing Fox tell you to return to the fort?" he added.

I stopped. "What about my duty to the ohwachira? My father and my mother's brother may lie injured or dead on that battlefield with no one to help them."

Tracking Wolf's eyes dulled with sadness. "We will go to them as soon as we can," he said, taking hold of my shoulders. "But you know better than I that we can't desert the Americans. We must tell Colonel Willett of our plans before we leave."

"You're right," I said.

I paused near the barracks long enough to replenish my ammunition and quench my thirst. When we reached the officer's quarters we hunkered down to wait for the chance to speak with Colonel Willett.

Hours later, daylight darkened to gloaming as the sun slowly dropped into her bed for the night.

Worry gnawed at my stomach as I lay down and pulled my blanket around me. "Where do you think they have carried the wounded?" I asked Tracking Wolf.

"Oriska," he said. "But not until it was safe for the warriors to return to the battlefield."

The voice of my father called my name. I turned away and swallowed the sob in my throat.

"The orenda will watch over them," Tracking Wolf said.

"We must find Willett at daybreak," I said. I rolled onto my back and stared up at the stars. I willed them to put out their lights and give way to the sun.

An Indian sharpshooter greeted the dawn by shooting the sentry on the northeast bastion. I jumped to my feet and peered up at the sentry box.

"I saw the shooter's smoke in yonder oak," a soldier shouted.

Tracking Wolf shook himself awake. "Did you see who got shot?"

"I don't know that soldier, but he's still standing."

"The sharpshooter must have lost his aim," Tracking Wolf said. "He usually drops them with one bullet."

The morning gun barked. Shot splintered the wood of the oak tree. The sharpshooter's body hit the ground with a sickening thump.

"That Indian is all done picking us off, boys!" Private Jones shouted. He picked up the sentry and waved him in the air. When hay sifted out of the sentry's uniform coat, the private laughed.[1] "I'm sorry to say, this man needs a new hat and more stuffing."

I threw back my head and laughed. Tracking Wolf slapped me on the back and whooped.

"Three cheers for Private Scarecrow!" Captain Jansen shouted.

I added my voice to the American cheers. My wounded spirit found pleasure in this good omen. I snatched a piece of hope and held it in my heart as I folded my blanket and chewed on some dried venison.

Soon Colonel Willett would come out of his quarters. With his permission, I would go to the battlefield and look for my family.

When the door finally swung open, I scrambled to my feet. Colonel Willett and his orderly strode past without even looking our way. They disappeared into Gansevoort's quarters.

A few minutes later the orderly emerged with a handful of papers and headed toward the officer's quarters at a brisk pace. I trotted to catch up.

"I must speak to Colonel Willett," I said.

He paused. "The colonel is very busy right now," he said looking distracted

"It's about yesterday's ambush," Tracking Wolf said at my elbow.

The orderly looked us up and down. "The loss of Herkimer and many of his militia in the ambush has hurt us sorely," he said. "Unless you have information about new reinforcements on their way to relieve us from this oppressive siege –"

"My father and uncle were with Herkimer," I said. "I need to go and look for them."

His eyes mirrored my fears. "My own father marched with Herkimer from Fort Dayton," he said.

"I will speak with Colonel Willett as soon as I can and bring you his answer."

Hours later, after a midday meal of dried corn and stale water, I joined Tracking Wolf and Jacob outside the garrison on the picket line.

The sun scorched my back as we watched and waited for the enemy to launch an attack. Shrill crow and jay calls warned of lurking danger. Did those same birds try to warn Herkimer and his men? Did our Oneida scouts sense danger before the ambush? I shook my head. If they had, they would have warned the Americans. They would have stopped them before they marched into the enemy's snare.

Sporadic enemy musket fire erupted and then quickly ceased. Only a few Iroquois sniped at us when we peered around a tree trunk.

"Why don't the British use their strength and advantage to launch an attack?" I asked.

"Look around," Jacob said. "Most of their

Indians have left the field. Without them they don't have enough men."

The British fired a small mortar at the fort. The Americans and Oneidas on the parapet fired back, sending whoops of laughter and catcalls along with each ball.

"With so little siege activity, Willett has no need for my services," I said. "I'm going to tell him tonight that I must go and search for my family."

Dusk fell with a heavy sprinkling of dew as we filed back through the sally-port. I reached the parade ground just as Colonel Willett's orderly stepped out from the colonel's quarters. I ran to catch up with him with Tracking Wolf at my side.

His face lit up when he saw me. "I've been looking for you," he said.

"Did Colonel Willett give permission for me to leave the fort tonight?" I asked.

The orderly frowned. "He said nothing is more important than holding this fort. He asked me to bring you to his quarters."

"I must go to my father and uncle tonight," I said.

Tracking Wolf snorted and shoved me forward. "First we will speak with Colonel Willett."

CHAPTER 20

ORISKA

Clouds hid the summer moon at the middle of the night. Except for sentries and posted guards, Fort Schuyler slept as Tracking Wolf and I painted our faces and readied our muskets. My heart raced as we loped to the sally-port. The three militia men who had come to tell of Herkimer's approach awaited us there.

"These men are experienced scouts," Colonel Willett's orderly said, pointing to us. "They will go ahead to find you safe passage to Fort Herkimer and Fort Dayton."

Lieutenant Helmer nodded in our direction. "We must get Colonel Gansevoort's message to the rest of the Tryon Militia. He needs every able-bodied man in this valley to help him hold out against the British."

I grunted. "We understand the importance of your message," I said. "If this fort falls, the Americans will not be the only people in this valley who suffer the consequences."

Willett's orderly followed us to the sally-port door. "There will be no record of your mission tonight," he said to us as the door swung open. "When you pass through that door you will be listed as deserters. That way, if you are captured, you can say you were spying for the British." [1] He turned to me and lowered his voice. "After these men reach Fort Dayton you have the colonel's permission to search the battlefield for your family."

I plunged into the sally-port with Tracking Wolf on my heels. We paused at the redoubt to allow our eyes to adjust to the darkness.

"The way will be treacherous until we get past the British and Indian camps," Tracking Wolf said. "We may have to walk in the Mohawk River to avoid them."

"We should take turns as forward scout," I said. "The one not scouting will guide the militia."

Tracking Wolf nodded. "The cry of a coyote will be our signal for danger," he said before he loped away. The darkness swallowed him up as the militia emerged from the sally-port behind me.

"Come!" I whispered, waving them to join me. I bent low and trotted toward the southeast bastion where the branch of the river ran closest to the fort. I looked over my shoulder, relieved to see that the three militiamen kept pace with me. I stopped and held up my hand when we reached the riverbank.

"Do not make a sound," I said. "We will follow this branch until we reach the great bend where it joins with the main river. We will go into the river there, where it flows between the British and Indian camps. You must remember to slide your feet as you walk through the water. Any splashing will alert the enemy. Once we make it past the camps we can follow the road south."

I held my breath as I led them on a twisting path through the tall, marshy grasses and cattails. My movements wedded with the evening breeze that rippled the lush growth near the river.

The Americans swished and jostled their way through the grasses and wild plants. I winced when their shoes squished through the swampy spots and clomped over rocks. Did they think the enemy had no ears?

The howl of a coyote shattered the night and curdled my blood. Was that Tracking Wolf or a real coyote? I signaled the militia to halt. At my sign we squatted down in the grass.

A few minutes later Tracking Wolf touched my elbow. "Many Indians prowl the forest tonight," he said. "I was accosted by a young Seneca warrior who warned me away from their camp. He said a council held soon after the ambush declared the Oneidas to be enemies of the Iroquois. They intend to send the bloody hatchet to our people."[2]

I shuddered. If we fell into enemy hands now, no quarter would be given. No restraint would temper their angry thirst for vengeance. I thought about my mother, Sweet Grass Weaver, and my sister, Two

Doves, and Polly – all of them alone at Kanonwalohale except for those too young or too old to fight.

"What have we done?" I said. "Those who insisted that we side with the Americans or risk the destruction of our homeland have brought us to the edge of the underworld where the Evil Spirit himself awaits our fall."

Tracking Wolf silenced me with his eyes. "There's no turning back," he said. "We must follow the road that we have chosen to its bloody end."

Scant moonlight sifted down between the dark clouds. I glanced at the Americans, huddled together in the brush by the riverbank. Clouds of mosquitoes circled their heads and dotted their faces and necks. I waited until Tracking Wolf led them down the bank and into the river before I trotted ahead to scout.

The night had waned by the time Tracking Wolf and his charges climbed up out of the river. I ran to meet them. "I saw a large group of Iroquois not far from here," I said. "They appear to be coming up from the lower valley to help the British."

"We can't risk an encounter," Tracking Wolf said. "Let's find a hiding place for the Americans until we can be sure that the enemy has moved on."

After we concealed the three militiamen behind some blown-down trees, we slipped behind a gnarled oak to keep watch.

Suddenly a terrible howl shattered the dawn. I peered around the tree half expecting to see a wolf trot out of the woods. I sniffed the air, but I didn't smell the sweaty pelt of a wolf. Instead, the early morning breeze carried a faint scent of death and decay.

Another shriek followed by an undulating moan resounded through the forest. That sound of that hopeless, overwhelming grief clutched my throat. Was it one of the wounded crying out for help, or someone mourning the death of a warrior?

I wanted to run to their aid but I couldn't abandon Tracking Wolf and the militia men. If we didn't deliver Gansevoort's message to Fort Dayton, Fort Schuyler would fall.

I shook my head to clear my mind. "We must be near the place of ambush," I said to Tracking Wolf.

Tracking Wolf put his hand on my shoulder. "That band of Iroquois must have passed us by now. They're probably headed back to the fort. I'll get the Americans moving. You can catch up with us after you scout the battlefield."

I clasped his hand in gratitude before I slipped into the forest.

A single voice cried out in mourning as I followed the nauseating stench of death onto a field of brutal slaughter. Silence draped the dead like a burial shroud. I swayed, overwhelmed by the horror that lay before me. Bodies of mutilated Americans and Indians sprawled across the ravine, some face down in a creek, others on their backs with staring eyes and gaping mouths. Many bore the wounds of the scalping knife.

I stumbled forward, scanning the faces of dead Oneidas. The brothers, Thomas and Edward

Spencer, lay close together in death. Other warriors had fallen here and there, wherever the fight had ended for them.

In the midst of the death and desecration, hope took wing in my soul. Eagle Tail and Laughing Fox were not among the dead. Nor did I see any sign of Jacob's mother and father. I whispered my thanks to the Great Spirit.

Suddenly a scream pierced the air. When I looked in that direction, a young Seneca gave voice to an undulating moan and tore at his shirt.

Red Jacket! I howled in sympathy as I trotted to him.

He looked up at me with tear-stained eyes. "My father!" he shouted. "They killed my father and it's my fault." He beat his chest with both fists and then bashed his forehead on the ground.

I touched his arm. "He was a warrior," I said. "Many brave warriors died in this bloody battle. It's not your fault."

He yanked his arm away. "I disgraced him!" he yelled. "This was my first chance to prove myself in battle. But when the Americans fought back, I ran away like a coward. I left him alone here to die."[3] He hid his face. His whole body shook with sobs.

After a few minutes he raised his head. He scowled and searched my face with angry eyes. "I know you," he said. "I saw you at camp when I was sick." His eyes narrowed. "Where were you when the battle started?"

"Spying on the Americans," I said, keeping my voice even.

"Have you been back to camp? Did you see what the Americans did? They looted and destroyed everything we had." His eyes darkened. He bared his teeth. "Today the Oneidas paid for their part in that treachery."

I held my eyes steady. "How did they pay?"

"We destroyed their village at Oriska this morning at daybreak," he said. "I myself slaughtered their cattle and helped burn their homes in honor of my father and all the brave Seneca warriors who lost their lives here." He threw himself over his father's corpse and moaned.

I shuddered. If my father and uncle were at Oriska with the wounded, had they been slaughtered as well? I backed away from his groaning cries and melted into the woods.

I ran to find Tracking Wolf and the militiamen. I stopped long enough to tell them what I had learned and then raced on to Oriska.

The smell of smoke and smoldering fire beckoned me. Charred and blackened timbers stood where once wood frame dwellings and longhouses had sheltered our people. Dead livestock littered the ground, their life's blood clotting in the dirt. Flames flared and smoldered in the corn fields. Bean and squash plants wilted on the bare ground, their exposed roots shriveling in the hot sun.

The whole village of Oriska, gone! I fell to my knees. Tears coursed down my face. The Hiawatha Belt of Peace had been destroyed, torn to shreds by the enemy's thirst for revenge. How could we ever make peace with those who did this to us?

The whole village of Oriska, gone!

As I scrambled to my feet, some women and children ran out from the woods, screaming and crying.

"Look at what they have done," one clan mother said. She pointed to a heap of dried corn mixed with dirt and smelling of urine. "They have killed our cattle and ruined our food stores. We will starve." Her eyes pleaded with me to do something.

Pity for her and the others squeezed my heart. "It's not safe for you to stay here," I said. "Go to my village at Kanonwalohale. You'll find food and shelter there."

I turned away as they began to gather up what was left of their belongings. I had to get back to Tracking Wolf and the Americans, but a sudden thought brought me to a halt. These women must have seen and tended to the wounded.

I turned back. "Did you see any injured Oneidas from the ambush?"

"Yes, many," the clan mother said, her eyes wet with tears. "Able warriors brought them here from the battlefield. We did what we could. They are on their way home, some to Kanonwalohale, others to old Oneida. Some will recover." She swiped at her tears. "Some will surely die."

I wanted to ask about my father and uncle, but what good would it do to know their fate? I already spent too much time searching and had learned nothing. For all I knew, my father and uncle might be home by now. Or, they might have been captured by the enemy and taken far away.

My shoulders slumped. In any case there was nothing more I could do. I had to guide the Americans to Fort Dayton before I could look for them. If I abandoned the Americans, I would not only dishonor my father, I would put my best friend and the militiamen in danger as well. And if they didn't make it to Fort Dayton because of my failure to complete this mission, Fort Schuyler and the whole valley would fall into the hands of the British and their Indians.

The village of Oriska was no more, the women and children who had lived there must seek shelter and charity elsewhere. I pitied them and their warrior mates who would howl in anger at the desecration of their homes.

I lifted my chin and raised my hand to the women in farewell. I made a silent vow to join the Oriska Oneidas when they went in search of revenge for this despicable act. But, for now, I had to stand with my father and the cause of liberty.

My heavy heart swelled with grief as I trotted back to find Tracking Wolf.

NOTES

TITLE PAGE

[1] Anthony Wonderly, "1777 The Revolutionary War Comes to Oneida County," *Mohawk Valley History*, Vol. 1, (2004), 15.

CHAPTER 1:THE SIGN

[1] "The Five Nations most likely banded together to form a league sometime during the latter half of the fifteenth century. . . . Iroquois storytellers described the formation of the league as the work of a Mohawk named Deganwi:dah [and according to some sources, Hiawatha] assisted by an Oneida named Odatshendeh (Quiver Bearer). . . . Odatshehdeh [Quiver Bearer] then persuaded his fellow Oneidas to join in the league of peace." Joseph T. Glatthaar and James Kirby Martin, *Forgotten Allies, The Oneida Indians and the American Revolution* (New York: Hill and Wang A division of Farrar, Straus and Giroux, 2006), 10-11

[2] "Letter from Col. Gansevoort to Col. Van Schaick: (July 28, 1777) Dear Sir: Yesterday at 3 o'clock in the afternoon, . . . The villains were fled, after having shot three girls who were out picking raspberries, two of whom were lying scalped and tomahawked, one dead, the other expiring, . . ." Edited with Commentary by Larry Lowenthal, *Days of Siege, A Journal of the Siege of Fort Stanwix in 1777*, (Eastern National, 1983, Third Printing 2005), 19

[3] "While it burned, the council fire symbolized that the Six Nations were of one mind; when the fire no longer blazed, it indicated that each of the Six Nations could freely decide its own course." Glatthaar and Martin, 134.

CHAPTER 2: THE KING'S MESSAGE

[1] "The Oneidas entered the war on the American Side when St. Ledger's army invaded Oneida Country to attack Fort Stanwix. As those British forces enveloped the Oneida Carry, an extraordinary meeting occurred between Paul Powless . . . and Joseph Brant, the famous pro-British Mohawk leader. The substance of their conversation (occurring sometime about August 2) was long remembered in Oneida tradition." Anthony Wonderley, "Revolutionary War Comes to Oneida County," *Mohawk Valley History*, Vol. 1, 34 -35

CHAPTER 3: THE FORT

[1] "A narrow space between the parapet and the ditch intended to prevent the earth from rolling into the ditch." Fort Stanwix National Monument, *Guide to Fort Structures*, National Park Service, (U.S. Department of Interior, GPO: 2005)

[2] "Whether a son of Hanyery was present [at the battle of Oriskany] is otherwise undocumented although one of them (Jacob Doxtater) is said to have fought at the fort." Anthony Wonderley, "Revolutionary War Comes to Oneida County," *Mohawk Valley History*, Vol. 1.,38

[3] "On August 1, . . . Colonel Dayton wrote to General Schuyler: 'The fort here which at present is very defensible against almost any number of small arms we had this day the pleasure to name Fort Schuyler.'" Alan E. Sterling, *Defenders of Liberty, Fort Stanwix During the American War for Independence* (Utica NY: Mohawk Valley History Project, 2005), 5

[4] "Under cover of darkness, Powless also got past the assailants. Like Two Kettles Together, he secured a horse and galloped all the way to Schenectady to warn patriot officials and seek help." Glatthaar and Martin, 158

[5] "Herkimer himself was serving under a cloud of suspicion. Some of his relatives had sided with the British, and his own brother, Joost Herkimer, was then under arms with St. Leger." Glatthaar and Martin, 161.

CHAPTER 4: WAR PAINT

[1] "Attacks generally took place at night or from ambush, with warning given by lighting an enemy house on fire." Moulton, 52

CHAPTER 5: THE RAID

[1] ". . . family lineage, called an owachira, the basic unit in the Oneida and Iroquois social structure", Glatthaar and Martin, 14.

CHAPTER 6: SURROUNDED

[1] "The citizens who comprised Herkimer's command were mostly farmers . . . Just to reach Fort Dayton, a large number of them had to travel substantial distances." Glatthaar and Martin, 160

[2] "A flag had to be contrived by the garrison as one had never been supplied. Ammunition shirts supplied the white stripes; the blue from a camlet cloak taken from one of the enemy in a battle near Peekskill; and the red stripes from miscellaneous pieces procured from the garrison. The flag flew on a pole set on the southwest bastion." Sterling, 8

CHAPTER 7: HOLD FIRE

[1] "A small party was sent out to the Landing to see if the enemy had destroy'd any our bateaus last night. This party found the Batteau man that was missing wounded thro the

brain, stabb'd in the right breast and scalped. He was alive when found and brought to the garrison but died shortly after." Edited by Larry Lowenthal, *Days of Siege,* 26

[2] "Aug. 3rd   About 3 o'clock this Afternoon the Enemy Shewed themselves to the Garrison on all Sides, Carry'd off some Hay from a Field near the Garrison, at which a Flag [of truce] brought up [by] Capt. Tice, came into the Fort with a Proffer of protection if the Garrison wou'd Surrender . . ." Edited by Larry Lowenthal, *Days of Siege,* 26

CHAPTER 8: FLAG OF TRUCE

[1] "Armed solely with a vainglorious pronouncement that St. Leger had plagiarized from Burgoyne, Tice urged Gansevoort to surrender . . . " Glatthaar and Martin, 159

CHAPTER 9: BESIEGED

[1] "This night we sent out a party and brought 2 stacks of hay into the Trench and set a House and Barn on Fire Belonging to Mr. Roof." Edited by Larry Lowenthal, *Days of Siege,* 28

[2] "Even as St. Leger's campaign settled into a traditional siege, the Oneidas inside and outside the bastion worked in concert with the rebels. . . . Oneidas . . . provided estimates about British forces under St. Leger . . ." Glatthaar and Martin, 172, 173.

CHAPTER 10: THE MISSION

[1] "Turtle taught us patience, never to give up. Seen as strength and solidarity, old and wise and well respected." Oneida Indian Nation – Culture and History, about our clans, http://oneida-nation.net/clans.html.

CHAPTER 11: AMONG THE ENEMY

[1] At Oquaga, Brant already had extensive connections, through his wife and children, his Oneida father-in-law, Old Isaac, and his many relatives and friends. . . . Glatthaar and Martin, 135,136

[2] Map: Iroquois Country and Oneida Towns, 1770s. Glatthaar and Martin, 50

CHAPTER 12: THE KING'S BATTLE

[1] "The 'new barracks' . . . were the creation of the French engineer who had supervised construction at the fort until July. . . . Partly as a result of the engineer's negligence, the fort was still raw and unfinished when the British arrived, and American work details had to make last minute improvements under enemy fire." Edited by Larry Lowenthal, *Days of Siege*, 29.

[2] ". . . St. Leger came forward with the main body of his command, estimated from 1,300 to about 1,700. This total included . . . approximately eight hundred Indians, mostly from the Six Nations." Glatthaar and Martin, 158.

[3] "By the 1700s it was suspended from a cord around the neck and hung on the upper chest area. Its function at this time was simply as a badge of rank for officers. The Indians wore cheap copies obtained through trade for decorative purposes, or were occasionally presented with 'real ones' by Americans or British to note exceptional service or leadership." Email received January 28, 2011from William Sawyer, Park Ranger, Fort Stanwix National Park, Rome, NY

CHAPTER 13: ATTACK!

CHAPTER 14: ESCAPE

[1] ". . . the Indians remaining at Stanwix surrounded the fort after dark and "commenced a terrible yelling . . . continued at intervals the greater part of the night." Watt, 135

[2] "This morning the Indians were seen going off from around the garrison toward the landing" Edited by Larry Lowenthal, *Days of Siege,* 29.

CHAPTER 15: STORM WARNING

[1] ". . . the British threw some bombs from their mortars. . . . The Indians were unimpressed with the Cohorn mortars, and later observed that their shells were like "Apples that Children were throwing over a Garden Fence." Watt, 133

CHAPTER 16: THE MESSAGE

CHAPTER 17: WILLET'S RAID

[1] According to the creation narrative: "Ultimately, the terrible struggle between good and evil takes place, a titanic contest for supremacy between the twins. Skyholder wins the battle and as his brother [the evil twin] sinks into the earth he becomes the Evil Spirit." Glatthaar and Martin, 9

[2] "Prior to Willett's approach, an Indian arrived at the Lower Landing and told Lieutenant Bird that Sir John was 'pressed.' Unaware that Johnson had returned to camp, Bird pulled his company from its post and briskly set off to reinforce the ambush." Watt, 191

[3] ". . . the baronet [Sir John Johnson], his family, and their guards fled to the riverbank with Willett's troops giving a 'fair firing' . . . while they were crossing the river." Watt, 191

[4] ". . . the camp was thoroughly plundered . . . and the letters taken from the militia at the ambush were carried off with a Grand Union Flag and four camp colors." Watt, 191-192

CHAPTER 18: WILLETT'S SCOUT

[1] "The 34th returned fire under this fierce response, but their musketry was 'very wild' and they soon panicked and 'scamper[ed] off" Watt, 194

CHAPTER 19: MY FATHER CALLED MY NAME

[1] "On the night of August 6, there had been some difficulty selecting a man for the dreaded northwest bastion's sentry post . . . a volunteer stepped forward. . . . before dawn, the fellow erected a scarecrow sentinel. . he then crouched behind the parapet . . ." Watt, 197

CHAPTER 20: ORISKA

[1] At midnight, Herkimer's three messengers, . . . slipped out of the fort to advise the lower Valley of the garrison's resolve to hold out. In the bustle of activity, two men managed to desert. Watt, 201

[2] . . . "a council of senior headmen . . . send a 'bloody hatchet' to the Oneidas to give warning that they were now considered an enemy" Watt, 196

[3] Not all the Senecas were eager for the fight. A youngster named Red Jacket and three other Genesee youths who were facing their first combat ran off when the firing began. . . .Watt, 163.

GLOSSARY

Bateau – Flat-bottomed river boat used to transport men and supplies.

Berm – A flat, grassy strip of land between the ditch and the fort wall that helped prevent dirt and stone from falling into the ditch.

Blatcop – Oneida warrior, Blatcop Tonyentagoyon of Oriska; half-brother of Hanyery Doxtator; fought beside the Americans at the Battle of Oriskany.

Captain Van Benscouton – 3rd New York Regiment, Continental Army; Commander of the advance guard during Willett's Raid.

Captain Bleecker – 3rd New York Regiment, Continental Army; Commander of the main body of soldiers during Willett's Raid.

Captain Gilbert Tice – A loyalist (an American who supported the British) officer who served with Butler's Rangers.

Captain Jansen (Janssen) – Captain in the 1st New York Regiment, Continental Army.

Chief Skenandoa (also Shenandoah) – Oneida chief and close friend of Reverend Kirkland; he supported the American's fight for liberty and actively participated despite his advanced age.

Colonel Gansevoort – Commander of 3rd New York Regiment, Continental Army; twenty-eight years old when he came to Fort Schuyler to hold the fort against the British.

Cornplanter – Indian name, Gayentwahga; Seneca Chief of the Wolf Clan; chosen one of two principal war captains by the Senecas.

Covenant Chain – An agreement between the British colonies and the Iroquois League.

Daniel – Fictional Oneida warrior, based on Daniel Teouneslees, son of Chief Skenandoah.

Eagle Tail – Fictional Oneida warrior, father of Walks on Snow.

Fighting Dog – Fictional Mohawk warrior.

Fort Craven – Construction began in the summer of 1756 near the future site of Fort Stanwix; the unfinished fort was burned that same August, along with Forts Williams, Wood Creek and Newport, by the British General, Webb, after rumors of a planned French attack on the carry.

Fort Dayton – Located north of the Mohawk River at German Flatts, Herkimer County, NY, about thirty miles southeast of Fort Schuyler.

Fort Herkimer – Located at German Flatts, Herkimer County, NY, south of the Mohawk River. Both the fort and the nearby Dutch Reformed Church (now called Old Fort Herkimer Church) were important in the defense of the Mohawk Valley. Built by General Herkimer's father at the onset of the French and Indian War, the church was fitted with over thirty gun ports.

Fort Newport – This fort guarded the Upper Landing on Wood Creek about two - thirds of a mile from Fort Stanwix, later Fort Schuyler. It was in ruins at the time of the British siege.

Fort Stanwix / Fort Schuyler – Built by the British in 1758; named for their commander, John Stanwix; renamed Fort Schuyler in honor of General Philip Schuyler by Colonel Dayton in August of 1776; never officially changed back, but in time it was called Fort Stanwix again.

Fort Ticonderoga – Built by the French in the mid 1700s; taken by the British in 1759, the fort was captured by

American soldiers Ethan Allen and Benedict Arnold in 1775; considered necessary to hold back the British Army, the fort was abandoned to the British in July of 1777.

Gorget – An officer's badge of rank for the chest that hung down from the neck. Gorgets given to the Indians were sometimes decorated with beads and quills.

Grand Council fire at Onondagas – The chief of the Onondaga tribe was appointed Fire-Keeper. All the tribes of the Iroquois confederacy or league came together at Onondagas to discuss any problems and renew their bond of peace.

Hanyery Doxtator – Oneida warrior, said to be the son of a German Palatine and an Oneida, or possibly Mohawk Indian; wounded at the Battle of Oriskany.

Hiawatha Belt of Peace – Made of white wampum beads; each bead stood for an historical event to be remembered. At the Grand Council it was placed on the ground in front of the Fire-Keeper with a white bird's wing. The wing was used to sweep dust and dirt away as a sign of removing any evil which could break the treaty of peace between the tribes.

Howling Wolf – Fictional Mohawk warrior.

Jacob Doxtator – Oneida warrior; son of Hanyery Doxtator and Tyonajanegen, also called Two Kettles Together.

Joseph Brant – Indian name, Thayendanegea; Mohawk Indian chief who served as a British Military Officer during the Revolutionary War and commanded some of the British Indians at the Battle of Oriskany. His sister, Molly, was the wife of Sir William Johnson.

Kanonwalohale – Oneida village about 17 miles southwest of Fort Schuyler; also called Oneida Castle; village of Walks on Snow.

Laughing Fox – Fictional Oneida warrior; brother of Sweet Grass Weaver; Walks on Snow's uncle.

League of the Haudenosaunee (also Iroquois League) – An alliance formed as early as the late 1400s, binding five tribes together in peace: the Mohawk, Oneida, Onondaga, Cayuga and Seneca. Later, the Tuscaroras were added as the sixth tribe. The name Haudenosaunee meant People of the Long House which gave an image of Five Nations living as a family under one roof.

Lieutenant Bird – British Lieutenant, Henry Bird, 8th Regiment, Light Armed Foot; sent ahead of St. Leger, with a fighting patrol of thirty soldiers, a squad from the 34th Regiment, and two hundred Iroquois warriors to seize the lower landing on the Mohawk River.

Lieutenant Colonel Marinus Willett – 3rd New York; helped defend Peekskill from the British before being assigned to help rebuild and man Fort Schuyler; second in command during the siege. He led the raid against the Loyalist and Indian Camps on August 6th.

Loincloth (also Breechclout) – A piece of clothing worn by men and boys; usually a long rectangular piece of tanned deerskin or cloth worn between the legs and tucked over a belt, so that the flaps fall down in front and at the back.

Major John Butler – British Indian agent and Commander of Indian Department Rangers (later known as Butler's Rangers), a battalion of loyalists who worked with the British Indians ; part of the blocking force sent by St. Leger to ambush Herkimer and his militia at the Battle of Oriskany.

Old Oneida – Indian name Ganaghaaraga; oldest, and most traditional Oneida village; by the 1770s had decreased in size and importance; located about 6 miles south of Kanonwalohale.

Old Smoke – Indian name, Sayenqueraghta; Seneca warrior of the Turtle Clan; chosen to serve as war captain with Cornplanter.

Oquaga – Oneida village; consisted of 4 towns on the banks of the Susquehanna River about 90 miles south of Kanonwalohale. Although Oneida, Tuscarora, Mohawk and Delaware Indians lived there, the Oneidas held leadership.

Oriska – Oneida village; now called Oriskany; located 7 miles southeast of Fort Schuyler; founded by Oneidas and Mohawks of the Mohawk Valley about 1765.

Orenda – The name the Iroquois called spiritual beings.

Quiver Bearer – Indian name, Odatshehdeh; persuaded his fellow Oneidas to join the League of Peace when it was being formed.

Paul Powless – Indian name, Tegauhsweaungaulolis; a young warrior from Oriska; may have lived at Kanonwalohale; his encounter with Joseph Brant is part of Oneida tradition.

People of the Standing Stone – Oneida people.

Polly Cooper – A young Oneida woman.

Private Jones – Fictional Continental soldier.

Red Jacket – A young Seneca warrior, at the Battle of Oriskany who ran home when the fighting began; in my story I had him come back after the battle.

Redoubt – An earthen and log wall built at chest height as a temporary barrier for defense; manned by armed soldiers from the fort to protect the sally-port entrance.

Reverend Samuel Kirkland – Presbyterian minister who came as missionary to the Oneidas at Kanonwalohale and traveled to all Oneida villages.

Royal Yorkers – A battalion of loyalists, later known as the Royal Greens; part of the blocking force sent by St. Leger to ambush Herkimer and his militia at Oriskany.

Sachem – Sachems were selected by clan mothers to serve as peace chiefs; three sachems were appointed for each clan: the Turtle, Wolf and Bear; the sachems met in clan council with counselors, clan mothers and selected elders to discuss and solve problems.

Sergeant Bailey – Fictional Continental soldier.

Sally-port – A postern or side –gate, or sometimes a subterranean passage, between the inner and outer works of a fortification; used by defenders to sally from or pass through.

Scalping – The removal of all or part of another person's scalp; first used in ancient wars in western Europe; in the early 1700s British colonial authorities offered money for Indian scalps; during the French and Indian War, both the French and British paid for enemy scalps taken.

Scalp Lock – (also Roach or Mohawk) A strip of hair, starting at the top of the head; sometimes decorated with feathers and quills.

Skyholder – The good twin in the Creation Story, he overcomes his twin brother's evil and drives him into the ground where he becomes the evil spirit; Skyholder and his grandmother, Sky Woman, ascend together into the Sky World.

St. Leger – British Colonel, Barry St. Leger; chosen by General Burgoyne to command the British attack on the Mohawk Valley.

Sweet Grass Weaver – A fictional Oneida woman; the mother of Walks on Snow.

The Carry – A portage road, one to six miles long, shorter when the water level in the Mohawk was high and longer when the water level decreased; boats and supplies were carried between the upper and lower landings on the

Mohawk and the upper and lower landings on Wood Creek to complete the water route between the Hudson River and Lake Ontario.

Thomas Spencer – Son of an Oneida mother and an American, he favored and assisted the American's fight for liberty. At the request of General Schuyler he traveled to Canada and brought back warnings of the planned British invasion; he and his brother, Edward, fought and died beside the Americans at Oriskany.

Three Rivers – Location of an Iroquois council meeting, west of Oneida Lake, northwest of Syracuse.

Tracking Wolf – Fictional Oneida warrior; friend of Walks on Snow.

Tryon County Militia – Made up of local males between the ages of 16 and 50, the individual companies probably gathered at their drill grounds and then marched to Fort Dayton and formed a brigade. Those who fought at Oriskany included: Colonel Ebeneezer Cox's First "Canajoharie" Regiment, Colonel Jacob Klock's Second Regiment drawn from the "Palatine" precinct, Colonel Frederick Visscher's Third "Mohawk" Regiment and Colonel Peter Bellinger's Fourth "Kingsland and German

Flats" Regiment.

Two Doves – Fictional Oneida child; sister of Walks on Snow.

Two Kettles Together – Indian name Tyonajanegen; wife of Hanyery Doxtator and mother of Jacob Doxtator.

Walks On Snow – Fictional Oneida warrior; son of Eagle Tail and Sweet Grass Weaver.

Wampum belt – Small polished beads made from shells, threaded on string and used for ceremonial purposes.

William Johnson – British Superintendant of Indian Affairs, he died before the Revolutionary War began. His actions, such as obtaining large grants of land for himself and his feud with Reverend Kirkland, may have influenced the Oneidas decision to support the American cause.

I WILL STAND WITH MY FATHER

BOOK TWO

By

IRENE UTTENDORFSKY

Walks on Snow and his fellow Oneidas press on in support of the Americans and their fight for liberty.

Will Walks on Snow and Tracking Wolf make it to Fort Dayton in time? When will Walks on Snow learn what happened to his father and his uncle at the Battle of Oriskany?

Yes, there is more to this story and you will find the answers to these questions and many more in Book Two. Read the short excerpt on the following pages.

CHAPTER 1

FORT DAYTON

I raced through the damp forest, tormented by the images of death and destruction that ran along with me. The faces of the women and children of Oriska haunted me the most. Their eyes had begged me not to leave them with no one to protect them and guide them to Kanonwalohale.

I clenched my fists. These were my people, my fellow Oneidas. I should have stayed, but duty made me turn my back on them. I had to guide and protect the Americans instead.

The morning sun poured its brilliance over the forest as I sped through the underbrush. Sunlight shimmered on mossy tree trunks and ancient, lichen covered rocks. I sent a prayer to the Great Spirit, asking him to walk with the women and children of Oriska.

Birds warbled sweet music to the new day. Their songs quieted my mind and honed my focus on the task ahead.

I leapt over a fallen tree and rounded a curve. A doe and two fawns plunged through the brush in front of me

I stopped and held my breath, straining to hear the noise that frightened the deer. The breeze carried no warning, so I knelt down and placed my hand on the ground. A faint rolling tremor tickled my fingertips.

My scalp prickled. Many feet silently walked the ground behind me. I sprinted off the path and dove behind a large rock. My heart raced as I waited for the first scouts to appear.

Were they Oneidas who had survived the ambush? They could be on their way to Fort Dayton after carrying the wounded home. My father and Laughing Fox might be with them. I raised my head and peered through the underbrush.

The first warrior rounded the bend, I ducked behind the rock. In the time it took to blink twice, my heart stood still. Then it jumped up to my throat and lurched back to life.

To be continued . . .

DISCUSSION GUIDE

Question	**Themes**

1. The Covenant of the Haudenosaunee or Iroquois League bound five, and later six, Native American tribes together in peace for hundreds of years. What is the name of the written document that binds the states of the United States of America in peace?

Government
Native Americans
Early Americans

2. Imagine you are an Oneida child in 1777. Your family and your whole village have decided to support the Americans as they fight for their freedom from the British king. Does that make you happy or sad? Why?

Change
Culture
Native Americans

3. Imagine you are an American child in. 1777. Your family and most of your friends are Patriots who have decided to join the fight for freedom from the British, but your best friend's father supports the king. Your father says he is a loyalists and vows to fight against him. Does that make you happy or sad? Why?

Change
Culture
American Revolution

4. How was family life for Oneida Indians and New York Americans the same in 1777? How was it different?

Family Structure
Civic Values
Daily Life

Question	**Themes**
5. Why was Fort Schuyler so important to the Patriot's cause?	Places and Regions
6. Why was Fort Schuyler so important to the British and Loyalists?	Places and Regions
7. Why was Fort Schuyler so important to the Oneidas?	Places and Regions
8. In what ways did the Oneida Indians help the Patriots during the Revolutionary War?	Spies Soldiers Communication Friendship
9. Why do you think the Oneida Indians chose to side with the Americans in the Revolutionary War, when most of the other Iroquois tribes supported the British king?	Government Civic Values Friendship Culture
10. How did the Revolutionary War affect daily life for Americans in 1777? How did the war affect daily life for Oneida Indians at that same time?	Change Culture Family Daily Life

ABOUT THE AUTHOR

Irene Uttendorfsky and her husband live in northern New York State. They are the parents of two grown children. For more information about the author and her books you may visit her website at www.ireneuttendorfsky.com, or become a fan on the author Irene Uttendorfsky facebook page.